## Her eyes twinkled. "Are you flirting with me?"

"If you have to ask I must not be doing it right."

She laughed some more. "I'm glad not everything about you has changed. You were always a great guy in my book."

Her gaze lifted up to meet his. The tender look in her eyes touched something deep inside him—a part of him that he'd thought was long dead. In that moment he felt more alive than he had in months.

Without thinking he reached out and caressed her cheek. "Thank you."

She leaned into his touch, short-circuiting the logical side of his brain. The only coherent thought in his head was to pull her close and kiss her. And this time he wouldn't be kissing her rosy cheek. This time he planned to find out if those cherry-red lips were as sweet and passionate as they were in his daydreams.

**Dear Reader**

When the idea for Jax and Cleo's story came to my mind I was enthralled with the idea of using Las Vegas as its setting. I find the history of that city—from the danger to the excitement—so unique. Vegas is full of action, and I wanted to bring a hint of that flavour into Jax and Cleo's story.

Cleo is a small-town girl searching for something to fulfil her, and she thinks she'll find it in this vibrant city. What she doesn't know and must learn is that fulfilment and satisfaction are things that come from within. And sometimes they're the things we've known all along but have forgotten or discarded as being not important enough.

Jax is drawn to Vegas as a means of escape, hoping to get lost in a crowd while enjoying the rush of excitement as he tests Lady Luck. What he doesn't count on is running into a blast from the past—his best friend's little sister, who isn't so little any more. But this unexpected reunion isn't the only hitch in his Vegas getaway...

Cleo and Jax are a great match as they challenge each other to conquer their fears. I hope you'll enjoy the mishaps and adventures on their journey to find their happily-ever-after.

Happy reading!

*Jennifer*

# THE RETURN OF THE REBEL

BY
JENNIFER FAYE

MORAY COUNCIL
LIBRARIES &
INFO.SERVICES

| 20 37 31 26 | |
| --- | --- |
| Askews & Holts | |
| RF RF | |

First published in Great Britain 2014
by Mills & Boon, an imprint of Harlequin (UK) Limited,
Eton House, 18-24 Paradise Road, Richmond, Surrey, TW9 1SR

© 2014 Jennifer F. Stroka

ISBN: 978 0 263 24264 5

Harlequin (UK) Limited's policy is to use papers that are natural,
renewable and recyclable products and made from wood grown in
sustainable forests. The logging and manufacturing processes conform
to the legal environmental regulations of the country of origin.

Printed and bound in Great Britain
by CPI Antony Rowe, Chippenham, Wiltshire

In another life **Jennifer Faye** was a statistician. She still has a love for numbers, formulas and spreadsheets, but when she was presented with the opportunity to follow her lifelong passion and spend her days writing and pursuing her dream of becoming a Mills & Boon® author, she couldn't pass it up. These days, when she's not writing, Jennifer enjoys reading, fine needlework, quilting, Tweeting and cheering on the Pittsburgh Penguins. She lives in Pennsylvania with her amazingly patient husband, two remarkably talented daughters and their two very spoiled fur babies, otherwise known as cats—but *shh*…don't tell them they're not human!

Jennifer loves to hear from readers—you can contact her via her website: www.jenniferfaye.com

**Recent books by Jennifer Faye:**

SAFE IN THE TYCOON'S ARMS
SNOWBOUND WITH THE SOLDIER
RANCHER TO THE RESCUE

**These and other titles are available in eBook format from www.millsandboon.co.uk**

# CHAPTER ONE

"YOU WON'T REGRET giving me this opportunity."

*And hopefully neither will I.*

Cleo Sinclair kept the worrisome thought to herself as she held her cheery smile in place. With the meeting at last over, she sailed out of the office of the vice president of player development, barely remembering to pull the door closed behind her. Away from Mr. Burns's cool demeanor and skeptical stare, she rotated her shoulders, easing the tension.

At the end of the hall, the elevator chimed and the door opened, allowing an employee to exit. Cleo stepped up her pace and slipped into the open car. Her pink manicured nail pressed the button for the main floor. Once the doors swished shut, the air whooshed out of her lungs and she leaned against the wall for support.

Step one was done. She had the job, albeit on a trial basis.

Now on to step number two.

She had to prove to the ever-doubting Mr. Burns that she was up to his challenge. She could and would bring in wealthy clientele eager to gamble at one of Las Vegas's most luxurious establishments, the Glamour Hotel and Casino.

A glance at her image in the polished doors had her adjusting her cheery yellow dress, which dipped a little lower than she'd like. When she'd worked in the accounting department, her attire hadn't been so important. But now working the front-end of the casino, everything about her appearance mattered. She smoothed her hands over the skirt. It wasn't the fanciest outfit she'd ever stitched. In fact, she'd worried that she'd made a mistake by choosing to wear it, but with each compliment from her fellow employees, her nervousness had eased… That was, until her meeting.

She halted her rambling thoughts and inhaled a deep breath.

It was too late to second-guess herself. The train had left the station. The ship had sailed. Oh heck, it didn't matter what phrase she used. Her plan was in motion. And she would succeed.

After all, she'd just put her entire future on the line. There was no going back. No changing her mind. If this arrangement didn't work, she couldn't stay in Vegas nor would she be able to return home to Wyoming.

The elevator doors silently slid open, revealing lush carpeting leading to the casino area. The soft lighting added to the ambiance while the blinking lights on the slot machines lured guests to try their luck at winning a fortune. Without windows or clocks, minutes stretched into hours. In fact, she had found herself losing track of time on the numerous occasions she'd spent on the floor training for this promotion.

A cheer echoed through the room and she glanced around to see an excited crowd at the craps table. The palpable energy charged the room. Someone must be on a roll of luck. She hoped this would be her lucky day, too.

As of yet, her whale, the big client, hadn't checked in. The VP himself would be greeting the guest and then he'd phone her when her presence was required. Her boss had gone over the guest's preferences, including his favorite game—blackjack. Her job was to keep the whale happy by comping his meals and getting him tickets to whatever shows he preferred. But the utmost important thing was to maintain this guest's privacy, above and beyond their normal discretion. Even she didn't know his name yet.

With her family's ranch deep in debt, this was her only chance to chip in and prove to them that she was still a Sinclair. And she was doing what any Sinclair would do—taking a necessary calculated risk and making sure it paid off.

She wanted to be close by, so she headed for the China Cup, a little coffee shop just on the other side of the reception area. Her mouth watered in anticipation of her first sip of a mocha java latte. Her steps came faster and when her blue suede heels hit the marble floor by the front doors, they made a rapid staccato sound.

A line of guests waiting to check in trailed past the sculpted fountain, blocking her passage. She paused, finding the line almost reached the entrance. They must be here for the car convention that opened today. It was the biggest event along the strip. The hotel had sold out months in advance. This would be an ideal time for her to fish for new clients—if only Mr. Burns didn't have her on such a short leash, insisting she cater to this one whale only.

"Hey, buddy," grouched a man near the front of the line, "how about moving aside?"

"Yeah," chorused a screechy female voice. "The rest of us have reservations."

Shouts and complaints rippled through the lushly decorated lobby.

Cleo glanced at the front desk to find one employee on duty. What in the world? There were supposed to be three people helping with check-in, but the only person standing there was Lynn, their newest hire. The girl was so green that she made the grass on the eighteen-hole golf course look dull and grayish. Why would they leave her alone at the front desk, today of all days?

"There has to be a mistake." Rising frustration laced the voice of the man standing at the counter.

But it was more than the angry tone that drew Cleo's attention. A note of recognition chimed in the far recesses of her mind. She craned her neck for a better look. Only the back of his short brown hair and his blue-and-white-striped collared shirt were visible. She knew that voice, but from where?

She glanced around, hoping to find someone qualified to assist the now flustered desk clerk. When Cleo didn't see any hotel employees moving in to help, she stepped forward. The least she could do was maintain crowd control until someone showed up to help with registration.

"Check again." The man's posture was rigid. "It's under Joe Smith."

"I am, sir." Lynn studied the computer monitor. "I can't locate your name in our system."

"Call your supervisor."

"I—I can't. She's just left. She's ill."

"Then call her boss. Surely there's someone around here who knows what's going on."

While Lynn frantically stabbed at the phone pad trying to reach someone to straighten out things, Cleo stepped up behind the disgruntled man. He didn't notice her as he leaned both elbows on the counter, peering at the computer monitor. Her gaze slid over his broad shoulders to his tapered waist, where his jeans accentuated his finer assets. Realizing what she was doing, she jerked her attention upward.

"Excuse me, sir. Can I help?"

When the man straightened, he was much taller than

she'd anticipated. As he turned to her, she found herself straightening her spine and lifting her chin. His assessing glance sent a shiver of awareness down her arms. She shook off the sensation. Obviously she'd been concentrating on the problems with her family and her job a little too much. It had been years since a man had such an effect on her. Not since...

Jax Monroe!

His cool blue-gray gaze met and held hers. The chatter of excited voices and the jingle of the slot machines faded into the background. Her breath caught as she waited for a sign of recognition. But none came. No smile. No hug. Nothing. What was up with that?

She smiled at him. "Hey, Jax. Still making trouble, I see."

He made a point of checking out the ID badge pinned to her chest. Was it just her imagination or was he taking longer than necessary to verify her name?

"Jax, it hasn't been that many years. You've got to recognize me."

Sure she'd changed some, but so had he. His long brown hair had been cut off. Her fingers itched to brush over the supershort strands. And his face was now pale instead of the tanned complexion she recalled—back when they spent most of their time outdoors.

But not everything about him had changed. If you knew to look for it, there was still a little scar that threaded along his jaw. She clearly remembered the day he'd gotten it. They'd been fishing at the creek. He'd been goofing off when he'd slipped and fallen on rocks. He'd clambered back upright and laughed at himself until she'd pointed out he was bleeding.

They'd practically grown up together...even if he was five years her senior. Hope Springs, Wyoming, was a very small town and it was great seeing someone from home.

It'd been so long since she'd been there. And her last visit had been such a nightmare—

Her throat tightened. Could that be the answer? It might explain why he was acting as if he didn't know her. Even though he'd left Hope Springs years ago, it was possible he kept in contact with someone from there. Her stomach churned. Did he know about what she'd done?

"Jax, stop acting like you could forget the girl who used to follow you to our favorite watering hole."

"I think you must have me mistaken for someone else." He turned his back to her and waited while the clerk spoke in hushed tones on the phone.

Mistaken? Not a chance. She'd know those baby blues anywhere. They could still make her heart flutter with just a glance.

Even with the passage of time and some outward changes, it was impossible he'd forget her. She'd had a teenage crush on him of megaproportions. To say she thought the sun rose and set around him was putting it mildly. She'd have done anything for him. She *had* done anything for him, including lying. So whatever he had going on with this alias of his, she refused to lie for him again. Not here. Not when she could lose her job and so much more.

"Stop acting like you don't recognize me. We need to talk—"

He glanced over his shoulder at her. His eyes darkened and his voice lowered. "No, we don't."

"Your name is Jax Monroe. You're from Hope Springs, Wyoming—"

"Stop." He turned fully around. "You aren't going to let this drop, are you?"

She crossed her arms and shook her head. When his eyes flared, she realized she'd made the wrong move. Her arms pushed up on her chest, which was now peeking out from the diving neckline. She wanted to change positions but stubborn pride held her in place. Let him look. Maybe now he'd realize what he'd missed out on when he'd brushed off her inexperienced kiss and skipped town without a backward glance.

Jax Monroe couldn't help but stare at Cleo—all grown-up and filled out in the right places. Long wavy honey-gold locks just begged for him to run his fingers through them to see if they were as soft as they appeared. Wow! If he had known how hot she'd turn out, he might have reconsidered returning to Hope Springs. After all, she'd had a crush on him that was apparent to everyone in their hometown… But then he recalled how young she'd been back then—much too young for him.

And now, as much as her body had grown and changed from the gangly teenager he'd once known, there were other parts of her that were annoyingly the same. She still spoke her mind at the most inopportune time and without any thought of who might be listening.

What in the world had made him think that flying across the country to hide in plain sight was such a good idea? On second thought, maybe he should have stuck it out in New York until it was time for his courtroom testimony. But he'd already made his choice. And now that he was here, he was looking forward to seeing if Lady Luck was still on his side.

Now if only he could just get Cleo to quiet down before she revealed his identity to everyone in the hotel. Frustration bubbled in his veins as he considered clamping his hand over her pink glossy lips. Then a more tempting thought came to mind of how he might silence her—lip to lip.

One look at the agitation reflected in her eyes and he knew she'd slap him if he dared kiss her. Definitely not a viable option, even if Cleo wasn't his best friend's kid sister. Kurt had been the one guy who'd always accepted him as is—the same guy who'd saved his bacon more than once when he'd acted out after his old man had called him a good-for-nothing mooch. The only thing Kurt had ever asked of him was to keep his hands off his little sis.

Jax smiled as he recalled Cleo with knobby knees, freckles and a long ponytail. Boy had things changed. She was smooth and polished like a piece of fine art.

Cleo's green eyes narrowed. "Am I amusing you?"

"Um, no." He struggled to untangle his muddled thoughts. "I take it by your name tag that you work here."

Lines creased between her fine brows. "What's the matter with you? Have you been drinking?"

"What? Of course not." He'd watched his father live his life out of a scotch bottle and the way his mother tried to please him, with no luck. Jax refused to follow in his father's unhappy footsteps. "I don't drink."

"So why are you calling yourself Joe Smith?"

"Let's talk over there. Out of the way." He pointed to the edge of the counter, away from the incoming guests.

She turned to observe the long line before following him. "I don't know what game you're playing, but I won't let you cause trouble here."

"Lower your voice." Luckily no one appeared to notice them or their conversation. The guests were more interested in the arrival of an additional desk clerk than in what Cleo had to say. "I promise you I'm not here for any nefarious reason."

"Why should I believe you? I covered for you when you 'borrowed' the school mascot and when you pulled those numerous other pranks. I know the trouble you can cause."

"You've got to trust me."

She arched a disbelieving brow. "Says who?"

Little Cleo had certainly gained some spunk. Well, good for her. It was also a relief to know she wasn't still carrying that crazy torch for him. The last thing he needed at this critical juncture of his life was more complications.

Her finger poked his chest. "You're up to something and I want to know what it is." Her tone brooked no room for debate. He wouldn't be wiggling out of this confrontation with some flimsy story. "You can start by explaining your need for an alias."

"Just leave it be."

She shook her head. "I can't look the other way. We aren't kids anymore. This is where I work and I can't let you jeopardize my job." Cleo's voice rose with every word. "But if you turn around and leave now, we can forget we ever saw each other."

He doubted he'd ever be able to wipe her sexy image from his memory. Her polished persona stole his breath away. She may have been a cute kid, but she'd grown up to be a real knockout. And as for leaving here now, he wasn't about to do it. He had as much right to be here as anyone else.

Cleo leveled her shoulders and tapped her foot. He hated to tell her but if she was angling for an intimidating pose, she'd missed her mark. She was more alluring than scary.

"Don't make me call for security."

Heads were turning in their direction. The very last thing he wanted was to become a spectacle for the masses. "You wouldn't do that to an old friend, would you?"

"A few minutes ago you didn't even know me."

He raked his fingers through his hair. Back in New York when he'd started receiving phone calls where the person at the other end wouldn't speak, followed by notes warning him not to testify, this vacation had sounded like the perfect plan. What could be better than getting lost in a crowd while testing his luck at the blackjack table?

Ever since the assets of his investment firm had been frozen by the government until the trial was completed, he'd missed the rush of working the stock market—the flood of adrenaline. He'd hoped Vegas would give him a similar high—a chance to feel truly alive again instead of living his life from one medical test to the next.

When his doctor gave him the green light, he'd picked a spot on the map far from New York and booked a plane ticket. He'd requested an alias be used while he was at the Glamour just as a precaution. But he had no idea how much of that he should tell Cleo. If only she would trust him…for old times' sake.

"What's going on here?" A short, round man in a business suit approached them. He glanced at Cleo. "Do you intend to interrogate all of the casino's important guests in the middle of the lobby?"

Her expression morphed from frustration to one of shock. Her gaze moved back and forth between the two men as though waiting for an explanation.

When none came, she said, "But he is—"

"Your client. And you will treat him with respect." The man turned to Jax and held out his hand. "Hello, Mr. Smith. I'm Mr. Burns. We spoke on the phone. Let's talk someplace a little more private." He led them to a hallway just off the casino's main floor and into an empty office. "I think there must have been some sort of mix-up. I'll see about getting you a new casino host."

Jax's gaze moved to Cleo. Beneath the makeup her face had taken on a sickly pallor. And her eyes held a deer-in-headlights panic. His initial instinct was to ride to her rescue. She'd always been the one to offer him a helping hand all those years ago back in Hope Springs. There was a strange satisfaction in seeing the roles reversed. But that was then, and this was now.

And it only complicated matters that he couldn't keep his eyes off this grown-up version of her. She was no longer too young for him. In fact, the reasons he had to keep her at arm's length became more muddled the longer he was around her. It was best to end things right here. After all, it wasn't as if the man was going to fire her over this.

# CHAPTER TWO

THIS COULDN'T BE HAPPENING.

Jax was her whale?

How was she supposed to have anticipated that? The last time she'd seen him, he barely had two coins to rub together. And now he was an important player in Las Vegas. How exactly did that happen?

Cleo's gaze shifted between the men. Neither of them seemed to notice that she was in the room. Did they think they could decide her future without even so much as consulting her? She wasn't about to let that happen.

"No other host is needed." Both men turned. She leveled a determined stare at each man before continuing to make her point. "Mr. Burns, you misunderstood what you overheard. Jax and I are old friends."

Her boss turned a questioning gaze to Jax. "Is this true?"

Cleo begged Jax with her eyes to back her up. After all, he owed her.

As the quietness stretched on, Cleo shifted her weight from one foot to the other. What was Jax thinking? His silence was even worse than any words he could say. She had to do something, anything, to keep from being canned for arguing with a MVP. Jax? A whale? The world could certainly be a strange place at times.

Cleo turned to face her disapproving boss. "We both come from the same small town in Wyoming."

Mr. Burns crossed his arms. "And do you always treat people from your hometown with such hostility?"

"I wasn't—"

Her boss's bushy brows arched. "I know what I heard."

"But you misunderstood—"

"Enough." Mr. Burns's hand sliced through the air. "I will deal with you later. Go wait for me in my office."

She hated being dismissed as if she was a child. She hated the thought of walking away with things unresolved, but she didn't want to make things worse… But then again could they get any worse? It was almost a certainty that when Mr. Burns joined her it would be to dismiss her. Not even a full day in her new position and she was being fired.

As she started for the door, her thoughts turned to her family. Even before learning of her family's financial problems, she'd made plans to transfer to the casino floor. She was bored senseless working in the accounting department. To think she left the family ranch because the work was isolating and she'd ended up taking a position where she spent her days alone in an eight-by-eight cubicle where silence was the status quo.

But then one day out of the blue her brother had called. She'd been so happy to hear from a family member. She hadn't heard a word from them since the funeral.

However, Kurt hadn't phoned with the intent of mending fences. He had news—bad news. The ranch was in arrears on its mortgage. And considering her Ivy League tuition was in large part the reason the ranch had been mortgaged in the first place, he thought she might want to help save their heritage.

The news totally blindsided her. Never once in her life had she imagined that the family had money problems.

And to know that she was about to be condemned for yet another Sinclair tragedy was not something she could let happen. She could not change the past, but going forward, she hoped to bridge the gap with her family.

Her fingers gripped the cold metallic door handle. One thought rose above the others: Sinclairs do not give up. No matter what.

Her grandfather had taught her that the first time she'd gotten thrown from a horse. If you wanted to succeed, you had to get back in the saddle and ride. That's what Sinclairs did—roughed things out.

She leveled her shoulders, released the door handle and turned. "Mr. Burns, you're right." His eyes lit up as though he was shocked by her bold confession. But before he could utter a word she rushed on. "Jax and I were having a disagreement. However, at the time I had no idea he was your special guest. I merely thought he was—"

"Here to check up on her for her big brother." Jax stepped between them to gain Mr. Burns's full attention.

At last, Jax found his voice, but why now? What convinced him to finally come to her aid?

The answers would have to wait. His motives paled in comparison to her losing her job and letting her family down…again. At the moment, she didn't have much choice but to go along with his fabricated story.

"That's right," she chimed in, trying to sound as genuine as possible. "And I didn't want Jax reporting back to my family about what I've been up to since moving away."

Surprisingly Mr. Burns's lips lifted at the corners as amusement danced in his dark eyes. "Let me guess, your family doesn't know that you've been working in a casino and they wouldn't approve of it."

This time she didn't have to lie. "That pretty much sums it up. They are old-fashioned in their beliefs."

Mr. Burns's eyes narrowed. "Then unless you're planning to find another job, I suggest you treat all of Glamour's guests with a pleasant demeanor."

She forced a smile on her face. "Of course. It was just a mix-up."

Mr. Burns turned to Jax. "The question still remains... Would you like me to assign you another host?"

He rubbed the dark scruff on his jaw. "No. Cleo and I will be fine. And we have some catching up to do."

Mr. Burns's gaze shifted between them as though making up his mind. "If that is your wish, Cleo will remain as your host. I have you set up in our most exclusive residence." He handed Jax the key card. "The bungalow should provide you with the privacy you're seeking. Cleo can show you the way. Do you need anything else?"

"Not at this time. I'm sure if something comes up Cleo will be able to take care of it."

Mr. Burns nodded. "But remember, I'm just a phone call away."

"Thank you." Jax extended his hand to the man.

After they shook hands, Mr. Burns moved past her, pausing long enough to say softly, "One more slipup and you're done."

A cold chill ran down her spine. The man had it in for her ever since the episode that occurred shortly after she'd started working in the accounting department. She'd pointed out some irregularities in his expense account, which were subsequently rectified.

Still, rumors were circulating that the only reason Mr. Burns had agreed to the promotion was because it was an all-or-nothing proposition. Either she was successful at endearing the high rollers to gamble at the Glamour Hotel and Casino or she was out on the street. And without a good reference, no other business on the strip would touch her.

"Don't worry. I'll make sure Jax is well cared for." She pasted on a smile, hoping it would suffice.

"I would expect nothing less."

The irritating note of superiority in Mr. Burns's voice grated on her razor-thin nerves. If the man hadn't been so eager to please Jax, she would be out on the curb right now. The fact she felt indebted to Jax ate at her.

With the door firmly shut, Cleo turned to Jax. Her mouth moved but the words wouldn't come. At last, she ground out, "Thank you."

His brows rose in surprise. "You're welcome. But the part I don't understand is why your brother didn't mention that you are working here in Vegas—"

"You've been talking to Kurt?" The thought left her unsettled.

Jax nodded. "We've kept in touch since I left Hope Springs."

Why was this the first she'd heard of it? Kurt was five years her senior, but she'd been closest to him out of all four of her brothers. When she'd needed someone to talk to, he was the one she'd turned to. So how had she missed hearing about Jax?

She tilted her chin and met his gaze. "You know, it's funny he's never mentioned you since you skipped town."

"Maybe he thought it was for the best."

"Why would he think that?"

Jax gave her a do-you-really-need-to-ask-that-question look. "As I recall, his kid sister had a massive crush on me—the kid from the wrong side of the tracks. I'm guessing he wouldn't want you having anything further to do with me."

Heat flamed in her chest and licked at her cheeks. "That was a long time ago. You can't fault me for my lack of judgment. I was just a kid. I've grown up since then."

"Trust me, I've noticed."

The implication of his words only multiplied her discomfort. Why was she letting him get her worked up? Back then she'd been a teenager with raging hormones and a complete lack of sense. And the fact that her family disapproved of Jax had only made him all the more attractive. What girl didn't go through a stage of falling for a sexy bad boy?

But even now with this mature version of Jax, his sexiness had only escalated. And his dreamy smile still had the power to penetrate her defenses and turn her insides to mush.

"We aren't here to talk about the past." She cleared her throat and schooled her facial features into what she hoped was a serious expression. "Why don't I show you to your bungalow?"

"Listen, I don't want to get you in any more trouble with your boss, but this arrangement obviously isn't going to work. So I don't care how you want to explain it to him, but you can't be my casino host. Better yet, don't say anything to him and you'll officially be my host but from a distance. A long distance."

"What?" Her chest tightened. "I—I can't do that. You're one of the casino's most valuable players. Upper management would find out immediately and accuse me of neglecting my duties."

"I don't need a babysitter." His brows gathered. "I just want a quiet vacation."

"And you'll have one while I take care of you...er, manage your needs." She pressed her lips together, knowing that with each attempt to dig out of this uncomfortable hole, she was only making it deeper for herself.

A deep chuckle rumbled from his chest. "Cleo, you still have a way of making me smile."

She glanced up, noticing how his face lit up when he smiled, easing his worry lines. Maybe his new life of luxury wasn't all chocolate and roses. From the obvious size of his bank account, she couldn't imagine what problems might be plaguing him. For a second, she considered asking but resisted. It wasn't any of her business.

"Does that mean I can go ahead and do my job?"

"Still as persistent as ever." Jax shook his head. "All right. Maybe we can try it on a trial basis. But that's no guarantee it'll work."

It was so much better than a no and it would give her time to soften him up. Hope bloomed in her chest. She would make this work…one way or the other.

Before she could say anything else to amuse him and embarrass herself, she turned to exit the office. "I'll show you around. I'm sure you're anxious to get to the tables."

"Actually there's no rush."

Cleo glanced back. "Really? Because if you're concerned about unpacking, don't be. I can have the staff do that for you."

"Are you that eager for me to start losing my money?"

Her gaze narrowed at his snide comment. "I get paid based on how much you wager, win or lose. So if you'll follow me, I'll give you a quick tour of the casino on the way to your lodging."

"That won't be necessary. I'd just like to get there quickly and discreetly."

If he wasn't up to something, why was he acting so strange? And did this have anything to do with his newfound wealth? The questions buzzed through her mind.

He was no longer Jax Monroe, Hope Spring's rebel. The truth was she never believed that he was a bad boy, more likely misunderstood and living up to people's low expectations of him. Back in the day he'd been so sexy with his long hair and holey jeans. Every girl in town had her eye on him—including her.

Cleo couldn't wait to tell her mother about this amazing transformation. Suddenly her excitement dipped. The gaping hole in her heart throbbed. Sometimes when she got excited, she'd forget that her mother was no longer speaking to her.

"Was there something else?"

Cleo glanced up at him, unable to recall their discussion. "What?"

"You were about to show me to my room." Jax's penetrating gaze met hers, making her turn away before she said or did something stupid.

"Follow me." She started toward the players' area.

"Is there a back way to my room?"

She nodded and turned around, guiding him down a long nondescript maintenance hallway. Jax may be tall, handsome and mysterious, but she had to remember that he was her client—a stranger to her now.

She didn't even know if she should trust him, but a little voice in the back of her mind said that he was still the same good guy down deep where it counted. He was also the guy her family didn't approve of—at least not for her. It niggled her that he was good enough for her older brother to pal around with, but when it came to her, she'd been forbidden to hang out with him—not that it had stopped her.

The silence between them stretched on. She didn't do well with awkward moments. "We're having a vintage car show in our convention center, if you'd like to look around—"

"Maybe later."

So much for conversation. She didn't recall Jax being this quiet when he was a kid. In fact, there were times he hadn't known when to shut up. She couldn't believe she was missing that smart-mouthed kid—the same kid who would go out of his way to put a smile on her face. What in the world had changed him so drastically?

She stopped and pushed open a heavy steel door. The glare of the Nevada sun nearly blinded her. She blinked and her eyes soon adjusted. As she moved along the secluded footpath, the sound of laughter, the cacophony of voices and the splash of water filled the air.

Jax grabbed her arm, giving her pause. "I thought we were taking the back way to my room."

An army of goose bumps raced over her skin. She pulled away from his touch and ignored the fluttery feeling in her chest.

She lifted her chin to face him. "We are. Your bungalow is in a secluded area just beyond the pool. Don't worry, there's a path over here on the side that we can use."

As they passed the pool she found herself glancing over at the crowd of young people on summer break, enjoying themselves. Her family were ranchers—and ranchers didn't take holidays. Or so her parents told her every time she asked them if they could go on a trip like her friends did.

It was always expected that when she wasn't in class, she would be at home helping out. It's what her brothers did. No one ever seemed to understand she was different. Was it so wrong to want to hang out with her friends? Or take vacations?

It was always presumed she'd become a rancher's wife—just like her mother and grandmother. After all, she was a Sinclair and ranching was in their blood. Except somehow the love of ranching had skipped over her.

"This sure is different from Hope Springs," Jax said, as though he, too, were thinking about the old days.

"Is that good or bad?"

"Neither. Just an observation."

The desert air was dry and hot as it rushed past them. Even though the private walkway was ensconced with palms trees, large rocks and various types of greenery, she gazed longingly at the glimpses of the enormous pool that had a wall of granite with a beautiful waterfall on one side. A dip in the cool water was so tempting. But employees were forbidden to indulge. She wondered if that rule could be suspended if someone like Jax invited her for a swim. After all, her priority was to keep her clients happy.

"What has you smiling?"

She was smiling? She hadn't realized that her thoughts had transferred to her face. She'd have to be careful in the future. The last thing she needed was Jax getting any ideas about her meandering thoughts.

"I was just imagining how nice it'd be to take a dip in the pool."

"It is hot out."

"It's always hot in Vegas."

"So how is it that the only Sinclair girl ended up in Las Vegas? I'd have thought you'd be back in Hope Springs with a cowboy by your side and a baby in each arm."

Cleo stopped short on the narrow path. He almost ran into her. "Not you, too. You sound like my parents."

"Calm down. I can see I struck a chord. I just thought that with your close-knit family that you'd never want to leave."

"Well, you're wrong. Besides, you did the exact same thing. I don't see you rushing back." She eyed him accusingly.

"That's different—"

"How?"

"You know I couldn't stay there." His posture grew rigid. "After my mother died, my father only got meaner. I wouldn't wish that life on anyone."

The pieces of the past started to drop into place. "That's why you were always out and about. You were trying to avoid your father."

Jax nodded. "It was easier than having to deal with him."

"But why did you have to play into the negativity by being at the center of all of the trouble in Hope Springs? How was anyone supposed to give you the benefit of the doubt when you never gave them a chance to trust you?"

His blue eyes stared straight at her. "Why didn't you write me off like the rest of them?"

"Because I saw there was more to you than you were willing to let on." She wasn't going to say that she'd had a bad case of puppy love. Thankfully they arrived at his bungalow, putting an end to this awkward conversation. "This is where you'll be staying."

She swiped her master key card and pushed open the door. When she stepped back to let him pass, he shook his head and waved at her to go ahead. "Ladies first."

She smiled. "Thank you."

So the bad boy had transformed into a gentleman. She definitely approved of this change. But that didn't mean she'd let her guard down around him. In her experience, people only showed you the side of them that they wanted you to see.

She'd been so foolish in the past, always looking for the good in people. She'd been too trusting—too understanding. And what had that Pollyanna attitude gotten her? A broken heart and being disowned by her very own mother.

In the end, people always let you down.

"This is nice," Jax said, drawing her back to the here and now.

"Yes, it is. It's our most private and exclusive residence on the grounds."

This was actually the first time Cleo had been inside

the bungalow. Only the most valued players were invited to stay here. And it was hard to believe Jax was now one of the elite. A man like that would not need or want for much.

But that still left her wondering, what was up with him using an alias? And his request for privacy was so different from the Jax she knew back in Hope Springs. In those days, he seemed to open his mouth just to annoy someone who was hassling him. Now he put thought into what he said and, more important, what he didn't say.

So what twist of fate had put him in her path? And why did it have to be him who held her future in the palm of his hand? Her stomach dipped. How did she get him to agree to keep her on as his host—permanently?

# CHAPTER THREE

JAX KEPT HIS eyes on the room and not on Cleo. Did she have any idea how irresistible she looked? How in the world did she think that they were supposed to spend time together with her wearing a dress that accentuated her curves? But then again she'd look good in anything, including a paper bag.

"Do you like what you see?" Cleo glanced at him from the entryway.

Oh, he definitely liked the view. Way more than he should. He cleared his throat. "Yes... Yes, I do."

Forcing his attention back to his surroundings, he observed the oversize leather couches. They looked inviting. He could easily envision settling in and watching a baseball game on the big-screen television. In fact, the idea sounded like something he'd enjoy indulging in right now.

Not so long ago, he used to work nonstop. But then he'd gotten sick and everything had changed. He had yet to regain his stamina after his medical treatments. It frustrated him to have to slow down, but until this court case was resolved there really wasn't any work he could do. This was his first vacation. He was curious to see if it was as great as people let on. Or if he ended up as bored as he imagined.

"If there's anything you're missing, just let me know and I'll take care of it for you."

He was positive the one thing he wanted, she would not supply. Not that he should or would act on the desire to taste her sweet lips. Cleo was the very last person he'd have a fling with. She deserved so much more—more than he could offer anyone.

"Would you like me to get you anything? Extra towels? Some food?"

"I don't think so. You can go." He didn't miss the frown at his dismissive tone and total lack of manners. His weariness was messing with his mind. "Thank you for showing me here, but I'll be fine on my own."

He turned his back to her and eyed up the couch. After a little television and some shut-eye, he'd be good as new— he wished. But with each day that passed, he was feeling a bit more like his old self.

Cleo firmed her shoulders. "I'd like to finish our talk about me staying on as your casino host. Perhaps we can come up with some sort of compromise."

He was intrigued. "What sort of compromise?"

She shifted her weight from one blue suede stiletto to the other, deciding just how much information she had to impart. Considering that not only her job but also the possibility of mending fences with her family was riding on her bringing in a large influx of cash, she had no choice but to be totally honest.

"I'd better start at the beginning." She worried her bottom lip as she sorted out in her mind a good starting point. "The thing is I sort of went over Mr. Burns's head to get this position and now he's out to get me."

Jax's eyes lit up as a smile tugged at his lips. "What do you mean sort of went over his head? You either did or didn't do it."

She hated how he put her on the spot. "Fine. I went over his head. But I wouldn't have had to if he hadn't kept passing me over every time there was an opening. And I'd already impressed his boss with a special project I'd previously worked on."

"Some things don't change." Jax laughed, remembering how he'd envied the way her father catered to her. He'd never known anything close to that amount of love. His own father had been too caught up in his own needs to worry about his son. The sobering thought killed off his laughter. "Why should I care about this mess you've gotten yourself in? I'm not the one who decided to buck the chain of command."

"So beneath that designer jacket and short haircut, you're still the tough, 'don't care' Jax, aren't you?"

"You don't know a thing about me." The fact that she didn't think he'd changed stung more than he'd expected.

"Then why don't you tell me how you ended up in this exclusive bungalow?"

He let out a frustrated sigh as exhaustion coursed through his body. "This is exactly why I need another host. I shouldn't have to explain myself. A stranger wouldn't butt into my life."

A pained look crossed her face, making him regret his heated words.

"You're right. You don't owe me any explanations. I just need you to forget everything that happened up until this point and give me another chance to be the best casino host you've ever had." She twisted her hands together. "But there's one more thing you should know."

His patience was wearing thin and he was so tired. "What is it?"

"This job isn't just for me." Her voice was so low, he almost missed what she'd said.

"What are you talking about?" Then a thought struck him. His gaze sought out her left hand, finding her ring finger bare. But that didn't mean she wasn't a single mother. "Who's relying on you?"

She wrapped her long honey-gold hair around her finger in a similar manner to the way she used to twist her father and brothers around her pinkie. But they were a long way from Hope Springs and he wasn't so easily swayed. If only he could get past his fascination with this grown-up version of Cleo. It was just a lot to take in at once.

"It's the ranch—the Bar S." Her worried gaze met his. "It's in a serious bind."

The worry in her eyes ate at him. "Kurt never mentioned anything about problems with the ranch when we've talked."

"I'm sure it's a matter of Sinclair pride. That's what got us into this trouble in the first place. It seems my father had been juggling money to cover his bases for quite a while without telling anyone that the Sinclair fortune had dwindled to nothing."

The knowledge that the high-and-mighty Sinclairs had come down off their lofty spot in the community didn't give Jax the satisfaction he once thought it would. Maybe it was the distressed look on Cleo's face that drove home the reality of what she was telling him. People were about to lose their way of life—their home.

"But I don't understand. What does any of that have to do with you being my casino host?"

"I need money to send home to put toward the mortgage. It's in arrears."

The Bar S was mortgaged to the hilt? He'd always looked at that ranch in awe and dreamed of one day having a spread just like it. Why hadn't Kurt mentioned any of this to him?

Later he would have to call Kurt and see if there was something he could do to help. Just as quickly, he realized he couldn't do that without mentioning Cleo. This would take a lot more thought before he acted. And right now, he needed to straighten things out with Cleo.

In his exhausted state, his brain just wasn't making all of the necessary connections. "So you want to be a casino host to make money for the family?"

She nodded. "The position pays a lot more than being an accountant."

He leaned back on the banister at the bottom of the steps. "Oh, yes. You mentioned making a percentage of what I wager."

She cocked her head to the side and stared at him intently. "Are you okay?"

"Of course. Why?"

"It's just… Oh, never mind."

This wasn't good. The last thing he needed was for her to figure out that something truly was wrong with him. It was difficult for him to maintain a normal existence while waiting for his test results without having to deal with the pitying looks or the sympathy.

"Jax, you have to do this. You owe me."

This sparked his attention. He always made it a policy to pay his debts. The thought of owing Cleo didn't sit well with him. At all. "I do? Since when?"

"Remember when I saw you on the day you left town? You asked me not to tell anyone what you were up to and I kept that secret for you."

Getting away from Hope Springs had turned his life around. If his father had his way, Jax never would have made anything of himself. Only his father hadn't lived long enough to learn how he'd graduated from college at the top of his class and had made a killing in the stock market. Not that it mattered. All of that, including Cleo, was in his past. And he wasn't going to get caught up in looking back—he didn't when his biopsy came back positive and he refused to look back now.

Oblivious to his inner struggle, Cleo continued, "I knew what you were running from and I wanted to help. If your father had known where you went, he'd have tracked you down and dragged you back. He'd have made your life miserable."

"You knew where I went? How?"

"I didn't know for sure. But I had a pretty good guess. You didn't talk about your family much, but when you did, you mentioned your mother's sister in Virginia. I figured that's where you went."

He nodded. "It is. I spent the summer with her before I went on to college."

"Your mother would have been so proud of you."

He grew uncomfortable with all of this digging around in his past. His mother had been sick off and on most of his life until her frail body finally gave in and she passed away when he was a teenager. No one ever spoke of her because very few people knew her since she was usually housebound from one ailment or another. The doctors would have him believe that she had a weak body, but he never believed that was what did her in. He was convinced her spirit had been broken by his father, who bullied everyone and ruled the house with an iron fist.

"I'm sorry." Cleo stepped closer to him. "I shouldn't have brought it up."

"It's okay. It's nice having someone else around who remembers her. You were always kind to her and she liked you."

"I liked her, too."

He remembered how Cleo would stop by the house with school fund-raisers. She never rushed off. She'd sit down with his mother at the kitchen table and chat. At the time he hadn't liked Cleo wedging her way into his life, but now looking back he realized she'd recognized a loneliness in his mom and had tried her best to fill it.

"Your mother was a really nice lady. And she made the most delicious chocolate chip cookies."

Before he could say more, his phone buzzed. Adrenaline pumped through his veins. At last, he'd know his test results. He glanced over at Cleo. "I'll be right back."

He moved to the kitchen, seeking privacy. No one knew about his brush with death, and he intended to keep it that way. He didn't want people looking at him as if he was less of a man.

He went to answer the phone but the other party had already disconnected. Jax rushed to check the caller ID but it was blocked, leaving him no clue as to who was trying to contact him. If it was important, they'd call back.

He returned to the front room, where Cleo was studying what was bound to be an expensive painting. He could never tell a Rembrandt from a Picasso. He just knew what he liked.

Jax stuffed his hands into his pockets. His fingers brushed over the smooth metal of the old pocket watch that he kept with him as a good-luck charm. More times than he could count it had brought him peace of mind. Only today its magic hadn't worked.

Today it reminded him of the past and the fact that Cleo's grandfather had given him the watch. Jax's gut was telling him that her grandfather would want him to help Cleo, no matter how hard it would be for him.

Cleo could feel Jax's presence before she heard him. She turned and noticed the dark shadows beneath his eyes. She didn't know what the man had been up to lately, probably too much. He certainly needed some rest.

"I'll get out of your way. But before I go, I'd like to confirm our arrangement."

Jax's brows rose. "I didn't realize we'd come to any agreement."

"Seriously, you're going to make me plead with you?"

He looked as though he were weighing his options. "You really want to put up with me for the next few weeks?"

Was he talking about catering to his every whim and desire? Her mind filled with the vision of him pulling her close and pressing his lips to hers. Okay, so maybe she hadn't totally outgrown her childhood crush. But fantasies were one thing. Acting on them was quite a different subject.

She'd learned her lesson about love. Men were to be treated with caution. She may date now and then, but she never let those relationships get serious. By dating the same guy less than a handful of times, she never let herself get close enough to risk her heart.

With Jax, it'd be a temporary arrangement—no chance for either of them to get the wrong idea about their relationship. "If you agree, I'll do a good job for you."

He glanced down at his phone as though expecting it to ring again. "In exchange, you'll keep my identity a secret. As far as everyone is concerned I'm Mr. Smith."

"I will make your privacy my top priority. But what's up with all of the secrecy?"

"Let's just say I'm on a much-needed vacation and I don't want anyone to disturb it."

"If you're supposed to be here for some R and R, you might consider turning off your phone. There's nothing so important that it can't wait. Why don't you let me reserve you a blackjack table for later today?"

Jax smiled and shook his head. "With your determination, I think you'll do quite well in your new position."

She straightened her shoulders. "I plan to."

He moved toward the couch and picked up the television remote. It was almost as if he'd forgotten she was in the room.

"Mr. Smith." When he didn't respond, she added, "Jax, if you're going to go by a fake name, you should at least answer to it."

He looked over at her. "I'm sorry. I didn't hear you."

"I'll make sure your line of credit is established and your table is ready. I'll be back as soon as everything is in place."

"There's no need to rush. I'll be fine."

"The fridge is stocked. Help yourself." She started for the door. Curiosity was eating at her. Something was troubling him and she was starting to worry about him. "Jax, just tell me one thing, are you in trouble with the authorities?"

"Why would you ask that?" He expelled a weary sigh. "You're still puzzled by the alias. Did you ever just want to get away? Want to be someone else for a little bit?"

Sure she had, especially after growing up in a small town where everyone knew everybody else's business. She used to daydream about the day she'd get to leave. The funny thing was the farther she got from her hometown, the more she missed it. Not the ranching part but the people.

And now that her father was gone and the ranch was in trouble, she felt as though she should be there to help out. But she wasn't wanted. The backs of her eyes stung as she recalled how her mother had told her to leave at her father's funeral, accusing her of being responsible for his death.

Jax stepped closer. "Cleo, what is it?"

She blinked back the unshed tears. "Nothing."

"You sure don't look like it's nothing."

"Well, you would be wrong. So we'll keep each other's

secrets. Yours from the rest of the world and mine from my brother. Deal?"

He frowned but nodded.

She slipped out the door. It was only then that she could breathe easy. Jax was here for more than just a vacation. Of that she was certain. He had a problem and if she had to guess, it was what had him looking so run-down. It must be something big and troublesome. But what could it be?

And why was she letting herself get drawn in when she had enough of her own problems?

# CHAPTER FOUR

WHAT HAD MADE him think a trip to Las Vegas was a good idea?

Jax grabbed a bottle of water from the fully stocked fridge. In the past two days, Cleo seemed to be everywhere he turned. It was almost as if she had him under surveillance. He paused, considering the possibility. Then realizing he'd watched too many spy movies after his treatments, he dismissed the idea. Even that would be too much for her.

The stress of waiting for his latest test results combined with a restless night had his imagination on overdrive. He really did need this vacation more than he'd originally thought.

The afternoon sun filtered through the sheers on the windows, casting a golden glow over the room. The couch beckoned to him. If he just sat down here for a minute, he'd be fine. Putting his feet up on the coffee table, he leaned his head back against the smooth leather upholstery and closed his eyes. This felt so good...

*"Jax."*

*He turned down a dark alley. Rapid footsteps sounded behind him. A gunshot pierced the night. He flinched. His legs moved faster.*

*He glanced around. The alleyway was empty. His heart pounded harder. No place to hide. No place to rest.*

*His muscles ached. His lungs burned. Still, he couldn't stop. He had to keep going.*

*"Jax."*

*The female voice was growing closer. Where were they? He couldn't see them. He had to keep moving, keep one step ahead of the man in black.*

*A brick wall reared up in front of him. He stumbled. Fell. Before he could get to his feet a hand clutched his shoulder.*

*He jumped.*

*"Jax, you're safe."*

One second he was in the alleyway and the next he was staring into the most amazing forest-green eyes. He blinked, trying to make sense of what was real and what was a dream. He jerked himself away from her touch and sat upright.

Cleo knelt down in front of him with concern etched across her face. "You were having a nightmare. Are you okay?"

"Um, yeah." He ran a hand over his forehead. "It's a bit warm in here."

She grabbed the cold water bottle from the coffee table and handed it to him. "Have a drink. I'll adjust the thermostat." She moved across the room and adjusted the touch pad on the wall. "Sorry I'm late. I had to pick my cat up from the vet."

"No problem. I wasn't in any rush." He raked his fingers through his hair.

The nightmares had started when he'd been diagnosed with cancer. With both of his parents dead at an early age, he didn't hold out much hope for himself. He'd lost count of how many nights he'd woken up with his heart racing and drenched in sweat, but back then the dream had been a blur. As time went by he remembered more of the details. Thankfully he didn't have them every night, only those times when his illness was weighing heavily on his mind.

"Are you sure you're okay?" She sent him a questioning stare. "I could call a doctor."

"What? Why would you do that?"

It was impossible for her to know about his medical condition. There were no loose ends for her to pull. No stones for her to turn. He got to his feet, stretched and headed to the minibar for a fresh bottle of water. He unscrewed the cap and took a long drink.

"If you're sick—"

"Why do you keep insisting I'm sick?"

"Because you're pale and perspiring. And obviously exhausted if you didn't hear me knocking on the door."

"It's just jet lag."

"Jet lag? Three days after the fact? I don't think so."

She had a point, but he kept quiet. Let her think what she wanted. He wasn't about to tell her that he'd just finished up a round of chemo and was now awaiting test results to see if he was in the clear or if the dreaded disease was still lurking within him.

"Maybe you should sit back down and take it easy." She fluffed a throw pillow before returning it to the couch.

He'd been taking care of himself since he was a kid. He didn't need her mollycoddling him like…like his mother used to do when he was sick. And this illness was not something that you shared casually over coffee. He could barely admit to himself the changes that had taken place in his life over the past year.

Now he just needed to be treated as if he was normal. And maybe then he'd start to feel normal, too.

She turned a sympathetic gaze his way. "I can get you some aspirin."

"Stop fussing over me." The hurt expression on her face had him regretting his outburst. She was only trying to be nice. "Thank you, but I'm fine."

Her brow arched as she pressed her hands to her hips. "If you're so fine, prove it. Let's head over to the casino and see if you can win back some of that money you lost yesterday."

Actually that sounded like the best suggestion he'd heard in a while. Because there was no way he was going to fall asleep again anytime in the near future. "Lead the way."

Surprise lit up her eyes, but for once she didn't argue. She turned on her stilettos and headed straight for the door. His gaze drifted to her derriere, nicely displayed in a red skirt that showed off her curves. He had no idea where she bought her clothes, but it was as if they were tailored just for her.

His throat grew dry and he gulped down the rest of the water. She'd certainly grown up to be a knockout. He couldn't believe Kurt let her out of his sight. If she was his little sister, he'd definitely keep her under wraps—away from men like himself.

Then again he wasn't anyone that her brother should be worried about. He was far from being classified as a ladies' man these days. That was one of the reasons he'd decided to come to Vegas—to distance himself from the stark reality of his diagnosis. Here he could be Mr. Smith—Mr. No Worries.

He rushed to catch up with her on the footpath. For just a bit longer he could hang on to the illusion that he was the man he'd always been—a man with a promising future. Now that future was littered with uncertainties.

"Have you lived in New York long?"

"Ever since I finished college." He glanced her way. "Did you move here after you graduated?"

Sadness filled her eyes and she nodded. "My family wanted me to return home. They'd even made arrangements for me to work for Mr. Wetzel in town, processing taxes."

"I take it that wasn't what you had in mind for your future."

She shook her head. "I thought I knew everything when I finished college. At last, I was free to make my own choices—to forge my own direction wherever it led me."

"It looks like you did well with those choices."

Her shoulders drooped. "Looks can be deceiving."

He concurred wholeheartedly. Things were never quite what they seemed from the outside. He was just sorry that Cleo had to learn that lesson the hard way.

"Hang in there. I'm sure life has some amazing things in store for you."

"We'll see."

The fact that she felt comfortable enough to open up to him warmed a spot in his chest. But he couldn't let himself read too much into it. She was probably lonely being so far from her family. And it wouldn't do either of them any good if he tried to fill that empty spot. It'd only make it that much harder to walk away.

"You know, I can be on my own today. I don't want to take up all of your time. I'm sure by now you have other guests to look after."

"Actually you're my one and only guest. Mr. Burns has me on a very short leash." Her cherry-red lips lifted and her eyes sparkled. "So name your pleasure and I'll make sure it's provided."

The sweet lilt of her voice and the sight of her tempting lips sent his mind spiraling back in time. He clearly remembered the one and only kiss they'd shared. He hadn't even seen it coming and it was over before he could react. The strange thing was that after all of these years, he had never forgotten that innocent moment.

He'd been kissed countless times since then and by experienced women who knew how to turn a kiss into an adventure. So why had the memory of those other kisses faded while hers stood the test of time?

Every detail of that moment stood out in his mind. He recalled how the morning sun peeked over Cleo's shoulder. The golden rays made her hair glisten, giving it the illusion of a halo. Her cheeks were rosy with color and her eyes sparkled like fresh-cut emeralds.

He'd been so mesmerized by the stunning image that he hadn't expected her to lift up on her tiptoes. Her gaze met and held his as she leaned forward. Her puckered lips pressed to his mouth. In the next heartbeat, she pulled away. And then, as if horrified, her eyes grew round. She'd pressed a hand to her mouth and run off.

The buzz of his phone drew him back to the present. At last, it had to be his doctor with the confounded test results. He glanced at Cleo. There was no way he was having this conversation in front of her.

He never wanted her to know that he had...Hodgkin's lymphoma.

He swallowed hard, still not comfortable with the "C" word.

He held up a finger to Cleo. "You can go ahead. I've got to get this."

He took a step back toward the bungalow. In fact, he took numerous steps before he pressed the phone to his ear. "Hello?"

Nothing but silence greeted him. Not again.

"Hello? Who's there?"

Frustration bubbled through his veins. Was it possible the anonymous phone calls were starting again just like in New York? But how had they gotten this number? He'd just had it changed.

He checked the caller ID. It was blocked. But then he noticed the reception bars were down to just one. The knot of tension in his gut eased. Perhaps the calls hadn't started again. Perhaps it was just a case of spotty reception.

His gaze moved to Cleo. She was standing next to a large palm tree. In the background was a glimpse of the waterfall at the edge of the pool. Her striking beauty drew him in. A year or two ago, he'd have tossed caution to the wind and lived in the moment.

But the here and now was all he had these days. He couldn't forget that. And he noticed the more time they spent together, the more he had to remind himself that he was in no position to offer her anything. His life was a continual question mark. And that was no way for anyone to live.

Her gaze caught his and held it. He found himself smiling back. Maybe he was thinking about this all wrong. Would it be a crime to let down his defenses just a little and enjoy Cleo's company?

It had been so long since he'd let someone in, even if it was just to kick back and chat over a meal. He longed for a little companionship. But he'd have to be careful around Cleo. She had a way of sneaking past his defenses. And he couldn't afford to let her get too close. They'd both end up hurt.

These thoughts made him all the more determined to check out early. Once he spent a little more time at the tables and made it look good for her, he was leaving Vegas.

He didn't know where he'd go, but that didn't matter. Still, it'd sure be nice to take a few happy memories of Cleo's smile with him.

Cleo stood next to a palm tree, wishing Jax would hurry up.

It was a hot day even by Vegas standards. Perspiration trickled down her cleavage. If this was going to take a while, she'd wait for him inside.

She glanced over at him and noticed how his brows were drawn into a dark line. And his eyes were narrowed as though he were upset. Something was definitely wrong. Should she go to him?

She stepped forward. Then stopped. It wasn't her place to interfere. As long as she saw to his needs while he was here at the Glamour, her job was done. Maybe once he got a few winning hands, it'd cheer him up.

Yet when he joined her, she couldn't help but ask, "Is everything all right?"

He smiled but the expression didn't reach his eyes. "Things couldn't be better. I'm on vacation and being escorted by the most beautiful woman in Las Vegas."

Without warning, he held up his phone and snapped her picture.

"What'd you do that for?"

He shrugged. "Why not? This way I have a reminder of my trip."

"You already had one from the other day."

His smile warmed her insides. "I could never have too many pictures of you."

His compliment caused a fluttering sensation in her stomach and silenced any further objections. Instead she returned his smile and when he offered her his arm, she gladly accepted. In a peaceable silence, he escorted her into the casino.

Inside, colorful lights twinkled while the murmur of voices filled the room. A group cheered at the roulette table. There were plenty of things going on in here to distract both of them. While Jax played blackjack, Cleo checked in with the pit boss to see if there were any new high rollers she could introduce herself to.

After all, Jax wouldn't be here forever. When he was gone and she'd proven herself, she'd need other clients. She may only be on a trial period right now, but she didn't intend for it to stay that way for long. And for her to be successful, she needed to plan ahead.

Sadly today there weren't any new leads for her. So after making the rounds on the casino floor, she gravitated back to Jax's table.

"And how are we doing?" She flashed him her practiced smile.

He didn't smile back. "Seems Lady Luck is on holiday."

"I predict things will turn around."

He cocked a dark brow at her as though gauging her sincerity before playing another hand. And losing again. Cleo's anxiety rose. If he didn't start to win soon, he'd quit. Or worse, take his business to another casino on the strip. Vegas was full of choices.

She wondered if that held true for her, too. At first, being a casino host seemed like an exciting challenge, but even though she was new to the job, she was finding that it didn't give her a sense of fulfillment, either. Now the only reason she wanted this job was to help her family get the ranch out of arrears. Once that was achieved, she knew she'd be moving on to something else. Because one thing she knew for certain, being employed in a casino didn't make her any happier than working on her family's ranch.

The most fun she'd had since arriving in this town was buying a secondhand sewing machine and returning to a hobby she enjoyed immensely—creating fashions. Her family may think her passion was a waste of time, but it'd saved her a bundle of money by allowing her to dress in style for a fraction of the price.

After the last losing hand, Jax turned to her. "That's it! I'm done. And don't say a word. No platitude or hokey prediction is going to fix this. I just hope you don't ever try to make a living off being a fortune-teller," he teased. "Because you're lousy at it."

"I—I'm sorry."

"I know how you can make it up to me."

"How's that?" She'd do it as long as it wasn't too over-the-top.

"Have an early dinner with me."

He was asking her to dinner? Excitement bubbled up inside her. She just as quickly tamped it down. He was her client. She had to stay focused.

"Thank you. But I don't date clients."

This brought an unexpected smile to Jax's face. "That's good because I'm not interested in a date. I just thought if you're going to follow me around, you might as well eat, too. But if you're not hungry that's fine."

"Oh." Her stomach growled. Heat filled her cheeks. Strike that. She was a lot hungry. "I'll join you if you tell me how you ended up going from ragtag jeans to designer ones."

His brows lifted. "You really find it so surprising that a person can turn their life around?"

"From what I've witnessed, people say they're going to change, but they're usually lying."

Jax stopped walking and turned to her. "Since when

did Hope Springs's very own Pollyanna become such a pessimist?"

She glared at him. "I was not Pollyanna."

"Oh, yes, you were. There was hardly a time you weren't smiling, and you seemed to think it was your job to make everyone else in town smile, too."

She hated that he still thought of her as some foolish kid with unrealistic expectations. "I grew up and found out that life isn't like in the movies. It doesn't come with rainbows and happily-ever-afters."

She started to walk again, not caring now if he followed her or not. Of course she'd always been smiling when he was nearby, it was how he made her feel. He surely didn't think she was that happy around everyone. But then again maybe it was best she didn't squelch his misconception. It was for the best that he didn't know those smiles had been just for him.

"Hey, slow down." He grabbed for her arm but she pulled away and kept on moving. "I didn't mean to upset you. I just miss seeing you smile and laugh. You're always so serious these days."

"I smile." She lifted her chin and pasted on a smile.

"I meant a real one. Not one of those practiced smiles you use for guests."

Cleo paused at the restaurant entrance, waiting for the hostess to seat them. She didn't know why she still let him ruffle her feathers. She really needed to loosen up.

The hostess seated them in the corner where there was dim lighting and a candle burning in the middle of the table. She inwardly groaned at the romantic setting. She glanced around, finding the restaurant empty, except for one gentleman across the room.

Jax leaned back against the cushioned bench as though the atmosphere didn't faze him. "So tell me about him?"

"About who?"

"The guy who made you stop believing in happily-ever-afters."

Her initial instinct was to tell him to look in the mirror. He'd been the first guy to break her heart. But she didn't dare admit it to him. He'd think she was being ridiculous. After all, she'd just been a silly kid.

But to this day she could still remember how crushed she'd been when she'd acted on impulse. She'd stood up on her tiptoes and kissed him. He hadn't kissed her back. He hadn't said a word. Not even a smile. In fact, all he did was stare at her. She'd been mortified.

The next time she saw him, he'd been leaving her grand-father's house. She'd run to catch up to him. She didn't know what she'd been expecting him to say, but it sure wasn't goodbye. Nor had she anticipated him leaning forward, kissing her cheek and saying, "See you, kid."

She'd been so devastated by him leaving town that she hadn't eaten her dinner and had hidden in her room all night. Luckily being the only girl afforded her the luxury of having her own room, where no one could see the tears she cried.

Jax took a drink of ice water and studied her over the rim. "Aw, see, I was right. It was a man who turned you into such a jaded person."

Cleo was not about to confess her long-ago teenage crush on him nor mention her college boyfriend, who got her to trust him—to believe they might have a chance at a future—before he two-timed her with her roommate. Some things were better not discussed.

"Let's just say I grew up and learned that people always let you down." She had to remind herself of that hard-learned lesson when Jax was around. With him it was too easy to fall into old patterns and let down her guard.

Throughout the meal they compared notes about college life and who had it worse. When Jax claimed he lived a semester with not much more than a can of tuna for his supper, he won hands down.

Since he'd started asking questions, it was time he answered a few. "Now, tell me more about your life in New York. You've said very little about what you do there."

"What can I say, I like to be a man of mystery."

Now that she couldn't argue with. He'd been a mystery for as long as she'd known him. He'd give just so much of himself before a solid wall would come up and block everyone out. She always thought that it had something to do with the way his father mistreated him. She inwardly cringed remembering how that man would call Jax rude names in the middle of town.

"Well, I hate to tell you this, but you aren't as mysterious as you seem."

"Really?" Jax propped his elbows on the table and leaned forward. "And what is it you think you've uncovered about me?"

"I know you work in New York City for some investment firm."

"So far you're right. I run a hedge fund on Wall Street."

"That sounds very impressive." She couldn't hold back a big smile. "I'm so happy for you. I just wish your mother was still around to see what you've done with your life."

"I think she would have approved."

"I know she would have. She was always proud of you." Cleo's thoughts filled with memories of the people of Hope Springs. "Do you ever think about going home?"

"This from the girl who moved to Connecticut for college and then graduated and moved to Vegas. I don't see you rushing back to Wyoming."

She shrugged. "I'm not cut out to be a rancher, even

if I am a Sinclair. I just wish I could have convinced my family."

"Ah, so you're off in search of yourself."

After all of these years it was as if he could still read her thoughts. Before she could tell him more, shouting came from behind her followed by the sound of shattering glass.

# CHAPTER FIVE

WHY NOW?

For the first time in forever, Jax had been enjoying himself. Instead of worrying about his test results or the upcoming trial, he'd taken time to enjoy a good meal and an easy conversation. Cleo was perfect, from her sparkling smile to the way the candlelight made her blond curls shimmer. This was the closest he could ever envision himself getting with a woman and he hated that the moment had come to an abrupt end.

Stifling a groan of frustration, he turned his head. A man stumbled to his feet while berating a young waitress as she set a cup on the table. The woman's face was splotched with color while all around her on the floor were shards of broken glass.

"I'll get security," Cleo said, scrambling to her feet.

Jax wasn't about to stand by and watch the scene unfold. He strode across the empty dining room, hoping to reason with the man. "Is there a problem here?"

"What's it to you?" The man slurred his words.

"It looked like you might need some help." He'd had his share of experiences with men in this guy's condition and knew they could be unpredictable.

"Yeah, get her to bring me another drink." The man's

bloodshot eyes glared at him and then turn to the young waitress. "I don't want this coffee."

"I'm sorry. I can't serve you any more alcohol," the waitress stammered.

Before the man could move, Jax situated himself between the two of them. He'd seen enough of this thing when he was a kid, when he was too young to do anything about it. Now he wouldn't just stand by and let a man take his frustration out on this woman.

"Why don't you try the coffee?"

"Fine." The man glared at him before grabbing a large brown mug from the table behind him. "If you're so interested in the coffee, you have it."

The next thing Jax knew warm liquid hit him in the face. His hands balled at his sides and a growl started deep in his throat. With every muscle tensed, he stood there soaked as coffee continued to drip from his chin.

"Enjoy." The man staggered away.

Jax took a step in the man's direction then stopped. More than anything he wanted to go after him, but he knew better. Nothing good would come from exacerbating the situation.

He glanced over in time to see Cleo standing at the entrance to the restaurant with two burly security guards. "That's the guy."

While security dealt with the obnoxious man, Jax turned to the waitress. "Are you okay?"

She nodded and handed him a towel. "Thank you. I don't know what I'd have done if you hadn't been here."

He proceeded to dry his face. "Glad I could help."

"I tried to make him understand that I have to follow the rules. I—I wasn't sure what to do. I'm new and no one has ever acted like that before. I should have handled it better." The girl grew flustered and he felt bad for her.

"You did fine. He was just a difficult man. Here, let me give you a hand cleaning up." He knelt down and started placing the big pieces of glass on the tray.

"If there's ever anything I can do for you, just ask for Marylou."

"Thank you." He flashed her a reassuring smile. "I'll keep your offer in mind."

Cleo returned with a mop and bucket. She looked him over. "Are you okay? Did you get burned?"

"I'm fine. Luckily the coffee had time to cool down. I'm just a little wet."

She gave him one last look as though to determine whether he was telling the truth. Then she started mopping the floor. The three of them worked together until the mess was nothing more than a distant memory.

"Well, hero," Cleo said, smiling up at him, "let's get you back to the bungalow and into some dry clothes."

He shook his head. "I'm no hero."

"Yes, you are. Just like all those years ago when you stood between me and Billy Parsons when he insisted I hand over my lunch money. You're still playing the modest hero. That's one of the things that I always—" She clamped her lips together and glanced away.

His black mood started to lift. "That you always what?"

"That I...I always admired about you."

The way she stammered around, he couldn't help wondering if that was what she'd originally intended to say or if there was some other hidden truth that was making her look so uncomfortable. He knew she had a crush on him way back then. And in all honesty, he'd thought she was pretty great, too. But way too young for him.

"Come on. Let's get you out of these." She tugged at his damp, clingy T-shirt. "Then again your new cologne, eau de coffee, might be a big hit with the ladies."

"You think so? How's it working for you?"

Her petite nose curled up. "I don't think it's your scent."

Her soft laughter was the sweetest sound he'd ever heard. And her smile started a funny feeling in his chest. If only he could keep her smiling.

Her eyes twinkled. "Are you flirting with me?"

"If you have to ask, I must not be doing it right."

She laughed some more. "I'm glad not everything about you has changed. You were always a great guy in my book."

Her gaze lifted up to meet his. The tender look in her eyes touched something deep inside him—a part of him that he thought was long dead. In that moment, he felt more alive than he had in months.

Without thinking he reached out and caressed her cheek. "Thank you."

She leaned into his touch, short-circuiting the logical side of his brain. The only coherent thought in his head was to pull her close and kiss her. And this time he wouldn't be kissing her rosy cheek. This time he planned to find out if those cherry-red lips were as sweet and passionate as they were in his daydreams.

His head started to lower when he heard footsteps behind him. He pulled away. Frustration bound up in his gut. He'd been so close—a breath away from satisfying his desires.

His hands clenched at his sides as he worked to compose himself. A little voice in his head assured him that this was for the best, but it didn't stop the wave of disappointment. Only a moment or two more and he'd have had a tantalizing memory to take back to New York.

"What's going on here?" Mr. Burns demanded. "Security said there was some sort of incident."

Cleo stepped forward. "Mr. Smith played hero. Everything is fine now."

Mr. Burns frowned as he surveyed Jax's stained shirt. "I'm sorry about that. Please stop by the men's shop and pick out a replacement. Charge it to my account."

Cleo clasped her hands together. "I can explain—"

"Trust me, you'll get your chance in my office. I have something to take care of first, but I'll be there shortly."

"Yes, sir."

Cleo's worried gaze moved from Mr. Burns to Jax. He wanted to reassure her that everything would be all right. That if he had to he would go over this man's head because he was really starting to dislike her boss and the tone he used when speaking to her.

Not wanting to do anything to make her even more uncomfortable, he decided to wait until she was gone before he had a word with this man. Then he'd set him straight.

Talk about a long, miserable evening.

Not even the magnificent sunset with its brilliant orange-and-pink glow could lift Cleo's spirits. She strode along the path to Jax's bungalow, grateful for its privacy. Her steps picked up speed as she continued contemplating what had just happened.

What made everyone think they knew what was best for her? First her overbearing family. Then her two-timing boyfriend. And now Jax...

She'd been a fool to think Jax was different—that he respected her ability to take care of herself. Even if it was to learn from her mistakes. She could just add him to her ever-growing list of people who'd disappointed her.

Her lips firmed into a line, holding back a string of heated words. She only had herself to blame. When would she learn to be more cautious?

There had only been one other time when she'd been this worked up—the last day she'd argued with her father on the phone. Her stomach churned as the chilling memory surfaced. She recalled how her father had yelled and then the phone had gone dead. Not knowing what had happened to him, she'd practically climbed the walls waiting for him to call her back. Nothing could ever be that bad. And thankfully this day wouldn't end with someone dying.

But before she was done, Jax would get an earful.

She stopped outside the bungalow and took a deep breath, trying to calm her racing heart. Her tightly clenched fist knocked solidly on the door. She waited. No answer. She once again pounded on the solid wood door.

"I'm not leaving until you talk to me," she shouted.

The door yanked open just as she raised her clenched hand.

"I think the entire resort heard you." He glanced both ways. "I'm surprised no one has come running to find out what's wrong."

She lowered her hand and marched past him into the bungalow. "Do you know what I just spent the last hour or so doing?" Without even waiting for Jax to respond, she motored on. "I had to justify exactly why I should continue as a part of the player development team. And Mr. Burns wanted to know if there was something going on between the two of us. Otherwise he just couldn't understand why you'd be so adamant about keeping me on as your host."

Jax closed the door and turned. "And, gee, I thought you came here to thank me."

"Thank you? If it wasn't for you, I wouldn't be in this mess."

"Hey, this isn't my fault. And as I recall, in the beginning I suggested another casino host take over."

The fact he was making perfect sense was not helping

matters. "Still, did you have to threaten my boss? He already dislikes me. Now he outright hates me."

Jax crossed his arms, his biceps bulging. "I didn't exactly threaten him."

She pried her gaze from his muscles and looked into his blue eyes, which were just as disconcerting. "Are you saying you didn't mention something along the lines of if he fired me, you'd take your business elsewhere? As well as that of your friends?"

Jax shrugged. "Someone needed to put that man in his place. He couldn't keep treating you like that."

"But that wasn't your responsibility. I can take care of myself. Stop acting like one of my overprotective brothers." She started pacing through the spacious living area. "I know how to handle men like Mr. Burns."

"Fine. Maybe I did come on a little strong, but that man is annoying. I don't know how you can stand working for him." Jax strode out of the room and quickly returned with some water. "Drink this. It'll cool you off."

She placed her sunglasses and phone on the table in the entranceway and accepted the tall glass. After a long sip, she said, "I know I should be thanking you."

"That's not such a bad idea."

She drew in a deep breath and leveled her shoulders. "I'm sorry. I shouldn't have blown up at you."

"Apology accepted."

"But you don't understand. My entire life my brothers have interfered with everything I do, never letting me stand on my own two feet. And my mother was constantly overriding my decisions. I thought that it was all behind me when I left Wyoming."

"I remember how your brothers policed every guy who looked in your direction. Did you ever have a date in high school?"

She nodded. "Mama finally put her foot down and made them back off on the couple of boys she approved of."

"But not the guys you had your eye on."

She shook her head. "You know how old-fashioned my family can be, and Kurt is no better. He doesn't understand why I had to get away to try different things and find what makes me happy."

"I guess I hadn't thought of it that way." Jax placed his hand over his heart. "I promise in the future to let you fight your own battles."

"Thank you. But you do realize once you check out, Mr. Burns will find a way to get rid of me."

"Are you saying that I have to stay here indefinitely?" Jax smiled, causing her heart flutter.

"Yes. But in order to do that, you'll have to start winning."

He rubbed his jaw. "I suppose you're right. Maybe we should go give it another try. I'm feeling lucky now."

"Are you serious?" There was still a chance of turning things around if Jax continued to test his luck at the tables.

The light from his smile snuck between the cracks in her dark mood and lightened her spirits. She was drawn to him, but she steeled herself against the desire. There was still so much she didn't know about him.

She'd never met anyone who could affect her so deeply. She'd come in here ready to tell him what to do with the job he'd secured for her, but instead she was walking out the door with a smile on her face, anxious to prove Mr. Burns wrong.

In the warm evening, the lights along the pathway gave off a soft glow. Jax was just behind her and she could sense his gaze on her. What was going through his mind?

Was he remembering how he'd almost kissed her in the restaurant? Drat Mr. Burns for ruining the moment. After all, it wasn't as though they were starting something serious. It would have been a simple kiss.

"It's a beautiful evening," Jax said from behind her.

"Yes, it is." But it wasn't the darkening sky or warm breeze that held her interest.

When Jax made another comment, she couldn't quite catch his words. Afraid she missed something important, she stopped short. He bumped into her. His hands reached and wrapped around her waist. She automatically turned in his arms.

Her gaze met his and her heart skipped a beat. "I didn't hear you."

"I said the sunset wasn't nearly as beautiful as you."

He was so close. She could smell his male scent combined with a spicy aftershave. A much better fragrance for him than the coffee.

Her good intentions evaporated as his intense gaze held hers. In his eyes, she detected mounting interest. She reveled in the fact that she could evoke such a reaction in him. She moved a little closer and heard the swift intake of his breath. He might fight it, but he was as attracted to her as she was to him.

Then she did something spontaneous. She lifted up on her tiptoes and pressed her lips to his just the way she had all those years ago. But this time she didn't stop there. She was no longer young and inexperienced. And she fully intended to make an unforgettable point.

Her lips moved against his very still mouth. Surely he couldn't be that surprised. This had started long ago and tonight she wanted to turn her fantasy into reality. So that when they each went their separate ways, she would have this memory to hang on to during those sleepless nights.

Her hands slid up over his solid chest and his muscled shoulders and wrapped around his neck. Her fingertips slid through his hair. With a moan, he tightened his hold on her, drawing her closer. His lips moved beneath hers. And like a timeless dance their mouths opened and their tongues met. Was it possible that this kiss—that Jax himself—was even better than she ever imagined in her dreams?

His kiss became frenzied with need. She met him stroke for stroke. His excitement increased her pleasure. Time slipped away. The only thing that mattered now was the man holding her.

Then as quickly as the kiss had started, it ended. Jax released her and stepped back. His breathing was as rapid as hers but his gaze lowered. He refused to look at her. What was that all about?

"That shouldn't have happened." He raked his fingers through his hair, scattering the short strands.

This was not the reaction she'd expected. She inwardly groaned. Why should this time be any different? He didn't want her. The acknowledgment stung.

"You're right." What had she been thinking? "It was my fault. It won't happen again."

She went to turn away when he reached out to her. "Hey, this has nothing to do with you. You're beautiful. Any man would be crazy to turn you down."

"You're making too much of it."

When would she learn to think before acting? Every time she put herself out there, she'd been rejected, first by her ex and then by her very own mother. People couldn't love her as is. They always wanted her to be more outgoing, more compliant, more something. There was always an area where she fell short in their eyes. She didn't even know what Jax found lacking in her and she wasn't about to stick around to ask.

She sucked down the bruising ache in her chest. It wasn't as though she still carried a torch for him. The kiss had been nothing more than a passing fancy, not something serious.

Swallowing hard, she levelled her shoulders and met his gaze. "I have some stuff to do. You can go ahead without me. I'll call and make sure your blackjack table is ready." It was then that she realized she didn't have her phone. "I must have left my phone back at the bungalow."

Jax turned as though to walk with her.

She held up her hand to stop him. "Just go into the casino. I'll get it."

He looked as though he was going to argue but then thought better of it. "Are you sure?"

"Yes. Go ahead into the casino. You should be all set up at the same table as earlier."

"Cleo, I'm sorry. I didn't mean to hurt you—"

She waved away his platitude. "I'm fine. It was a mistake kissing you all those years ago and it was a mistake tonight."

His mouth opened but she didn't wait around to hear anything he had to say. She strode away, completely mortified by the way she'd thrown herself at him. What in the world had gotten into her? She'd like to blame it on a full moon, but there was none. This mortifying disaster was all her fault.

When she arrived at Jax's bungalow, she realized her pass card was with the phone locked inside. She expelled a sigh. Just what she needed now was to tell him that she had forgotten not only her phone but the hotel pass card, as well. Could she look any more incompetent this evening?

The sound of footsteps had her taking a calming breath. A shadow fell over her. She turned, expecting to find Jax, but instead a tall, muscular man dressed in a dark suit stood before her. The stranger was built like a linebacker and under different circumstances this might have intrigued her, but tonight she didn't want to be bothered.

Her gaze rose to his face. She was caught off guard by his dark, menacing eyes. "I'm sorry but this is a restricted area. Are you a guest of the hotel?"

The man's tanned face creased with an intimidating frown. "I'm looking for someone. A Jax Monroe."

She had no idea who this man was or who had pointed him in this direction, but the first rule about being a casino host was abiding by their client's wishes. And Jax had no wish for anyone to find him here.

"I can't help you. Did you try at the front desk?" She knew that they wouldn't release guest information, but she hoped this man didn't know that and would go away. "Maybe they can give you some information."

"Just tell me where I can find him."

An uneasy feeling inched down her spine. Was this the man Jax was avoiding? If so, she fully understood why Jax wouldn't want anything to do with him. Her mouth grew dry. The guy looked as though he could bench-press a car. And the menacing look in his eyes gave her the creeps.

Something definitely wasn't right here. Her palms grew moist. Standing alone with this man was not a good idea. It was time to get moving.

"I really need to be going. I have people waiting for me." She started walking, but instead of taking the private path back to the casino, she veered toward the pool, hoping there might still be some stragglers hanging out.

"Don't walk away from me. This is important. Just tell me where to find him and there won't be any trouble."

She didn't need to hear any more. She walked faster. The man easily kept pace.

The hairs on the back of her neck lifted. When she reached the pool area, luckily some young people were still milling about. Not that they were paying her any attention. Still, whatever this man meant by his threat, he wouldn't be foolish enough to try something with so many witnesses... Would he?

She got as far as the first line of lounge chairs when his meaty fingers reached out and clamped around her upper arm, halting her progress. She jerked her arm, but his grip was like a vice. Her heart jumped, lodging in her throat.

He pulled her to him. Her back pressed to his chest and he wrapped his hand over her mouth. "I want you to give Jax a message—"

Cleo bit down on the man's finger.

A curse thundered in her ears. He yanked his hand away. Never taking her eyes off him, she backed up. He lunged for her. In the ensuing struggle, her foot got caught in a lounge chair. She lost her balance and fell backward, hitting the concrete.

# CHAPTER SIX

"OPEN YOUR EYES."

Jax stared down at Cleo's pale, lifeless form on a stretcher in the back of an ambulance. His chest tightened as he said a silent prayer to the big guy upstairs. She just had to be all right. She had to be.

His thumb stroked the soft skin of her limp hand. He had no idea what had happened. When he'd heard there was a commotion out by the pool and Cleo hadn't returned, he'd gone looking for her. He never expected to find Cleo in a crumpled heap on the ground.

There hadn't been time to stop and ask questions. All he could think about was her opening her beautiful green eyes again. But one thing he knew in that moment was that the girl who'd given him a peck all those years ago still meant the world to him. He reached into his pocket. His fingers traced over the pocket watch—his good-luck charm. He was about to pull it out and press it into her limp hand when he noticed her fingers move.

"Jax? Where am I?"

Cleo's voice was weak but clear. He'd never heard anything so wonderful in his whole life. He longed to pull her into his arms and hold her close.

"You fell, but don't worry, you're going to be fine now." She tried to sit up, but the straps on the gurney held her down. "Not so fast, they still have to check you out. You got quite a bump on your head."

She glanced over, noticing the paramedic reading off her stats to the hospital.

"My leg hurts and I can't move it."

"They immobilized it. Looks like you banged it up pretty good."

She closed her eyes and he worried that she had slipped into unconsciousness, but she quickly opened them again. "I'm sorry to be such a bother."

He held her hand between both of his and gave it a re-assuring squeeze. "You could never be a bother. Right now all you have to do is concentrate on getting better."

He wanted to ask her what happened, but now wasn't the time to get into it. Still, Cleo wasn't a clumsy person. When you lived on a ranch, you learned to be fast on your toes. So what exactly had happened to her?

He was still holding her hand as they backed up to the emergency room entrance. Her fingers were cold as she kept a firm grip on him. When he tried to pull away, she wouldn't let go.

"It's okay. They'll take good care of you." He stared straight into her eyes, noting the worry reflected in them. He lifted her hand and pressed his lips to her delicate skin. "You're safe now. I promise."

"Will...will you stay?"

"You bet. They couldn't drag me out of here if they tried."

"Thank you."

The fact that she wanted him with her, that he was able to provide some sort of comfort, stirred a strange sensa-tion in his chest. It wasn't the protective feeling of a big brother watching over a little sister. No, this was something different—something much deeper. Much more powerful.

The scare had been of a magnitude that he'd never experienced before. He didn't know where the feelings came from or what to do with them—he just knew his place was right here by Cleo's side.

The ambulance doors swung open and they rushed her off. He wanted to go with her—to make sure that nothing happened to her. But as he started to follow Cleo's gurney, a nurse stepped in front of him and pointed the way to the waiting area, promising they would notify him when he could see her.

Frustration knotted his gut. The last time he'd let her out of his sight something bad had happened. But Cleo was safe now. She was in the hospital. Doctors and nurses would be seeing to her needs.

He entered the spacious waiting area lined with rows of black cushioned chairs. He took a deep breath as the reality of his location struck him. It wasn't so long ago he'd been the patient. Even though it had been a different hospital, the memory had him on edge. He didn't want to be here—not at all.

But he'd promised Cleo he'd stay. He wouldn't break his promise to her. It was the least he could do for her. He tried sitting but that lasted all of thirty seconds. He paced the length of the room. Back and forth. He wasn't the only one wearing a concerned expression. The waiting area was filled with young and old people all waiting for word on a loved one.

"Excuse me, Mr. Monroe."

He turned to find a police officer. "Yes."

"I'm here about the incident at the Glamour. Did you see anything?"

The police were involved. This wasn't good. "No, I didn't. I was inside and heard about the commotion by the pool. I went to investigate and that's when I found Cleo. Do you know what happened?"

"I'm still piecing things together. We have a report of a man getting into a scuffle with Ms. Sinclair and your name was mentioned."

"Have you talked with her?"

"Not yet. That's where I'm headed next."

Dread dug at Jax as he wondered if it had anything to do with his mysterious calls. "There's something you should know."

The officer turned his keen, observant eyes on him and listened intently as Jax revealed how he was a key witness in a federal money-laundering case. He also mentioned the strange phone calls that had started in New York.

The officer asked a few more questions, jotted out some notes and gave Jax his contact information. "If you think of anything at all that might be helpful, let me know."

"I will." And he meant it. He wasn't going to take unnecessary chances with the woman he…he…cared about.

Whether he liked it or not, she was definitely getting to him. She was making him feel things that he didn't have any right to feel. The only way to stop this growing attraction was to follow through with his plan to leave Vegas. He eyed up the exit. But he couldn't break his promise to her. He'd wait until he saw her and was certain she was going to be fine.

Almost a half hour later, a nurse stood at the security door that led into the examination area. "Mr. Monroe, you can come back now."

When he came to a stop next to Cleo's bed, he was stunned by what he saw. A white bandage was wrapped around her forehead. Her face was nearly as pale as the sheet. And her injured leg was elevated. He didn't know what he'd been expecting, but it wasn't her looking weak and helpless.

She studied him. "Do I really look that bad?"

He'd obviously let his poker face slip again. Still, the sight of her lying there injured had shaken him more than he'd anticipated. "Sorry. I wasn't expecting to find you all bandaged up."

"Jax, there's something I need to tell you—"

"And how's the patient?" A male voice came from behind him.

Jax turned to find a doctor in a white lab coat standing at the opening in the curtains surrounding the bed. He glanced back at Cleo. "We'll talk later. I'll just wait outside."

"It's okay." She grabbed his hand. "You can stay for this."

The doctor cleared his throat. "Ms. Sinclair has a mild concussion. We're still not certain about the extent of damage to her leg. I'm waiting on the films. However, I want to keep her in the hospital under observation. She was unconscious for a bit and I want to make sure there aren't any complications. But she's insisting that she's going home."

Jax turned to her. "You need to listen to the doctor. He knows what he's talking about."

"I'm not staying." A stubborn glint reflected in her eyes. "I can't sleep in hospitals. Besides, I feel fine now."

"She can go home as long as she isn't alone," the doctor said while looking directly at Jax. "Can you stay with her?"

"I don't need him." The sincerity in her pointed words poked at Jax. "I can take care of myself."

The doctor's brow drew together. "I'm sure you can in most cases, but you've got a serious bump on your head and you need to stay off your leg as much as possible. So either you stay here and let the nurses look after you or you can go home with…"

"Jax. Jax Monroe. And I'll see that she's taken care of."

Cleo worried her bottom lip. And in that hospital gown, she looked like a child again. All he wanted to do was take care of her any way possible…even if it meant getting closer to her instead of beating a trail into the sunset. That would have to wait for another day.

Cleo's worried gaze turned to him. "Are you sure about this?"

"I wouldn't have said it otherwise."

The doctor's gaze swung between the two of them, deciding if he could trust them. "Now that it's settled, I'll go check on things. If you wait in the lobby, we'll call you when she's ready to go."

Jax didn't mind a few minutes to himself to pull his scattered thoughts together. He started for the doorway when Cleo grabbed his hand.

"I need to talk to you. I just remembered something."

"Don't worry. We'll have plenty of time for that later."

"But this is important." Her distressed tone caught his attention.

He wondered if this had something to do with the police poking around. "I'm listening."

"There's a man after you."

"What?"

As though recalling her fingers were still gripping his hand, she let go and made a point of straightening her white sheet. "When I went back to the bungalow a man approached me. He wanted to know how to find you."

"And he attacked you?"

"Not really. When I tried to get away from him, he followed me. He grabbed my arm and put a hand over my mouth. He said he had a message for you."

Alarm arrowed through Jax's chest. "What is it?"

Cleo's gaze lowered. "I don't know. I bit his finger before he could relay the message. He let go of me and the rest is kind of a blur."

His gut was telling him trouble had followed him from New York. And Cleo had ended up paying the price. Guilt beat at his chest.

"Don't worry. He won't bother you anymore."

"How do you know? Who is this man? What does he want?"

Jax held up his hand, halting the flow of questions. "I don't know him, but I promise you won't have to deal with him again. Remember from here on out I'm in charge of your safety. Doctor's orders."

She started to sit up. "Jax, I need to know what's going on."

"Calm down." He placed a hand on her shoulder, pressing her back against the pillow. "When I learn something I'll tell you. Now I have a couple of phone calls to make."

Jax hated the thought that he'd dragged Cleo into his problems. He had no proof that this mystery man was tied into the money-laundering case, but he'd be willing to bet his fortune that he was right. His priority now had to be keeping Cleo safe. And since that hired thug knew her name, her face and where she worked, it wouldn't take long for him to track her down at home, either.

Just then the doctor returned. "We'll have you fixed up in no time."

That was Jax's cue to leave. He turned back to Cleo. "Don't worry. I'll take care of everything."

As he strode away, she called out, "What are you going to do?"

He didn't pause to answer because, at that moment, he didn't have a clue. It was obvious that he needed to get Cleo and himself out of Las Vegas. But how far could he take her with her injuries? If she needed further medical attention, he didn't want to be stuck out in the middle of nowhere. There had to be a compromise. A place where the thug hired to scare him into silence wouldn't think to look for either of them.

*Free at last.*

Cleo settled back against the leather seat of a large SUV. Even though her hospital stay had only lasted a matter of hours, for her it felt like days. And now Jax was playing the dutiful hero and riding to her rescue. She had no idea where he got this sweet ride, but she appreciated its spaciousness more than she could say.

"Thank you. But you really didn't have to go to such lengths. I could have called a taxi to take me back to my place."

"I don't think so. Remember I'm the one who promised the doctor I'd take care of you."

At the next traffic light, he turned left instead of right.

"You went the wrong way. Wait. How do you know where I live?"

"I don't."

"It's the other direction. I live at 331 Villa Drive, apartment C3. You can just turn left up here and loop around." When he kept going straight, she sat up a little straighter. "Where exactly are you taking me?"

"Do you always ask so many questions?"

She glared at him. "I demand to be taken back to my apartment."

"Not today. We're going someplace where you can rest and not worry about any unwanted guests."

"But I can't." She didn't like the sound of this. "I have a job...er, at least I hope I still have a job."

"Of course you do. You were injured on Glamour grounds while performing your duties. Therefore you're entitled to workers' compensation. Not even Mr. Burns would be foolish enough to let you go and face a lawsuit."

The medication they'd given her at the hospital was making her head woozy. "The doctor said it wouldn't be long until I could get around."

"And until then you need to rest as much as possible. Now just relax. I've got everything under control."

"How am I supposed to do that when you won't even tell me where we're going?"

"We aren't going far. Just north of the city. And I promise you'll like the accommodations."

He was trying to sound upbeat, but she knew he was worried. "You think that guy is going to come back, don't you?"

"He won't bother you where we're going."

She wanted to believe him, but she didn't even know what he was mixed up in. The adrenaline that had been driving her drained away, leaving her feeling wiped out. She was with Jax. Nothing would happen now because the one thing she did know was that she still trusted him. She instinctively knew that he'd protect her.

She leaned her head back, fighting to keep her eyes open. The image of her kitty came to mind. She'd called her neighbor Robyn McCreedy to check in on him. Still, it wasn't the same as being there, especially since he'd just been neutered.

"I can't stay here long. I have to get home."

"Don't worry. I'll get you home soon." Jax glanced over at her. "You can sleep. I'll let you know when we're there."

She really shouldn't trust him so easily, but her eyelids felt so very heavy. If she could just close her eyes for a minute, she'd be all right...

"Cleo, wake up. We're here."

Her eyes snapped open, not recognizing her surroundings. The bandage around her forehead was getting itchy so she rubbed at it, wanting to take it off. But the doctor had warned her to leave it on until the stitches on the back of her head had a chance to heal.

She gazed up at a large gate that was automatically opening for them. "Where are we?"

"Someplace safe."

Jax maneuvered the vehicle between the gates and down a road lined with jaw-dropping mansions. It was dark out, making it difficult to see the details of each impressive estate until they pulled into the driveway of a humongous home. She'd only ever seen something this extraordinary in glossy magazines.

Soft rays from the full moon bathed the white stucco home, giving it a magical glow. And it was two…no, wait, make that three stories high. With the lights on inside, it looked like a gem against the velvety night. Its sweeping length and elegance left her in awe.

"I hope you won't mind staying here."

She blinked, making sure that it was real. "Mind? It's amazing." Then she turned to him. "Is it yours?"

He shook his head. "I don't have any use for a place this big. It belongs to a friend of mine."

"That must be some friend. Is he famous?"

Jax chuckled. "You might say that. Remember the movie from last summer, *Shooting Stars?*"

"You mean the Western romance? I think everyone went to see it, including me. It was a great mix of action and passion."

"My friend will be glad to hear you're such a fan."

"He filmed it?"

"No, George starred in it."

Cleo's mouth gaped as she sat there trying to process

this information. "No way. Are you totally serious? He's drop-dead gorgeous."

Jax smiled and shook his head. "I do believe you're starstruck."

"Did you see the movie?" She fanned herself. "He's so hot. In the film he was the marshal and he was on the hunt for train robbers. He ended up rescuing the heroine from a train accident the robbers had caused. It was so romantic how he cared for her and kept her safe."

Jax cleared his throat. "I'll be sure to tell George when I talk to him. Now, is there any chance you want to go inside?"

"And see the rest of his house? You bet." She reached for the door.

"Wait! I'll help you. We don't need any more accidents tonight." He alighted from the vehicle and circled around to open her door.

"But how did you get George to lend you his house?"

Jax gave a nonchalant shrug. "It's not his primary residence. He spends most of his time in Hollywood."

"I still can't believe he's letting us stay here."

"Let's just say that he owed me a favor and I called it in. George is a really good guy. He was happy to do it."

"Did you tell your friend that we are on the run from some ape?"

"Ape, huh?" Jax smiled. "I'm glad to see your sense of humor hasn't been injured."

She thought back to her run-in with that man and a shiver ran down her spine. "I just refuse to give him power over me by calling him a big, mean, scary dude…even if he was one."

Refusing to dwell on what happened, she turned her attention to the long sweeping steps that led to the front door. And then she glanced down at her leg. This was going to be a challenge, especially when she wasn't used to getting around on one good leg.

But before she could ask Jax for the crutches, he scooped her into his arms. Her body landed against his solid chest. He'd definitely filled out in the years they'd been apart.

"What are you doing?"

"Taking you inside."

Her hand automatically slipped around his neck. "But I can manage—"

"Do you have to argue about everything?"

She pressed her lips shut. If he wanted to carry her up all of those steps, why should she complain? She wasn't feeling exactly steady on her feet. Tomorrow would be plenty early enough for her to prove her independence, even if she had to be aided by those confounded crutches.

Her head rested on his shoulder as he moved up the steps. Beneath the moonlight with the warm breeze swirling around them, it would be so easy to let her guard down. If she closed her eyes and inhaled his masculine scent, she could let herself get swept up in this very romantic scenario. Not that she had any intention of making a fool of herself again. If there was any more kissing, it would be Jax who made the first move.

One night here and then she'd return to her apartment to finish recuperating. Being situated in the middle unit of a young people's complex, tenants were coming and going at all hours of the day and night. She wouldn't have to worry about being alone. They'd be around if she called out for help. Yes, that would work. One night with Jax and then they'd go their separate ways.

Her thoughts turned back to Robyn, who was more than a neighbor—more like the sister Cleo never had. It was nice to have someone in her life now who cared. She'd told Robyn that she'd be home sometime that night. She really should let Robyn know that her plans had changed. She didn't want her to needlessly worry. Cleo reached for her phone but realized she didn't have it.

"Jax, I left my phone back at the bungalow."

"It's for the best."

"What? But I need my phone. How am I supposed to contact people and let them know that I'm okay?"

"They'll just have to wait. Phones have GPS tracking units in them. It's possible that thug could track us down that way. Don't worry. I got a disposable phone for emergencies."

The hairs on the back of her neck lifted. "Jax, how much trouble are you in?"

# CHAPTER SEVEN

ALONE AT LAST.

Jax gently lowered Cleo down onto a long white couch in the expansive living room. He regretted having to let her go. There was something so right about having her slight figure curled up next to him. It'd taken every bit of willpower to concentrate on climbing the stairs instead of turning his head and kissing her.

His gaze dipped down to her lips while remembering how sweet they'd tasted. This wasn't right. He should be worried about the man who'd run into Cleo at the hotel, not contemplating repeating their kiss because the one they'd shared earlier had been far too brief. And even worse, it had left him anxious for more of her touch.

He'd never had a woman distract him to this extent. What was so unique about Cleo? Could it be the fact she'd always been forbidden fruit? After all, she was one of Hope Springs's highly respected Sinclair clan whereas his own family had been barely tolerated.

The attraction appeared to be all one-sided as Cleo sat up and looked around the expansive room. "Did you see those posters in the hallway? This really is an honest-to-goodness movie star's house."

"Are you saying you doubted me?"

Her gaze darted around the room. "Look at the mantel. There's an award. Do you think he'd mind if I touched it?"

"I don't see why he would have to know." When she went to stand, Jax placed his hand on her shoulder. "I'll get it for you."

"Can you believe we're here? And look over there." She pointed to the wall to the left. "There's pictures of him with actresses and politicians. Look at that one of him with the president."

Jax chuckled at Cleo's awestruck face. He retrieved the gold figurine, surprised to find it was rather heavy, and handed it to her.

"I just can't believe you're friends with him. Can you get me his autograph?"

"I'm sure that can be arranged. Now sit there and don't move. I'll be back."

"Wait." She looked up. "You promised we'd talk."

"And we will right after I get our stuff. Just enjoy checking out that award."

The events of the day were catching up to him, and he couldn't wait until he got Cleo settled in bed. He inwardly groaned at the thought of her stretched out on some silky sheets. He gave himself a mental shake. That wouldn't and couldn't happen. Being a total gentleman tonight was going to be a feat all of its own.

Jax made a few trips to the car and deposited the final items next to the couch.

Cleo eyed up the stash. "What is all of that?"

"Things you'll need while we're here."

"But both of those bags look full. What did you buy?"

He handed over a shopping bag and she peered inside. Her lips formed an O and he realized too late that he'd given her the pink bag. Still, the color filling her cheeks matched the bag and made him smile.

"Don't worry. I didn't pick out the lingerie. Marylou helped me out."

Cleo's thin brows rose. "Marylou? You mean the woman from the restaurant? The one you rescued from that rude guy?"

He nodded. "She said that if I ever needed anything to ask. I couldn't risk going back into the Glamour and I didn't want to risk going to your place, so she discreetly picked up some of my things from the bungalow and bought you some essentials at the guest shops."

Cleo grimaced and adjusted her leg. "You're making this sound like we're going to be here for more than just tonight."

He glanced at his watch, realizing it was time for her pain medication. "We are. But don't worry. I have plenty of groceries."

She sat up straight. "I can't run off with you. I have responsibilities. People who will be worried about me."

"Listen," he replied as he got to his feet, "I'm not any happier about this than you are. But until the police track down this guy, we're staying put. Now it's time for your pain meds. I'll be right back."

"Jax, you're being ridiculous. I can get these things for myself."

He headed for the kitchen, ignoring her protest. Why did she have to be so stubborn? Couldn't she relax and let him take care of her? Did everything have to be a struggle?

He returned quickly, handing over the glass and the medication, which she took without so much as a comment. He sank down into the armchair across from her and folded his arms behind his head.

"You have to admit staying here won't be so bad." He was trying to convince himself as much as her. He leaned his head back. One by one the muscles in his body relaxed. "Even the furniture is comfortable."

He closed his eyes. This was the most relaxed he'd been in a long time. Was it the house? Or was it the company—Cleo's company—that had him thinking about the here and now instead of the uncertainty of his future?

"I'm still waiting."

Her voice startled him as he started to doze off. He lifted his head to look at her. "Waiting for what?"

"For you to explain why we're here. Who's the ape that's hunting you?"

Jax ran a hand over the evening stubble trailing down his jaw. "I honestly don't know who the man is. But the police are on it now. With the aid of the surveillance cameras at the casino, they'll be able to identify and locate him."

He hoped.

"But you do know why he's here and what he wants." Her eyes grew round. "Jax, what did you do?"

The fact she thought he might be on the wrong side of the law dug deep into his chest and pulled at the old scars on his heart. Years ago, when all of Hope Springs saw a delinquent kid, she'd looked at him as somebody worth befriending. Cleo always made him feel as though he mattered.

But for the first time, the look in her eyes had changed. Was she now looking at him as her mother had done and seeing him as the no-good Monroe kid who could never amount to anything but trouble. Anger and hurt churned in his gut. He thought he was far past these old feelings—yet being here with Cleo had rolled back time.

"I'm not a criminal," he ground out.

Color filled her cheeks. "I—I didn't mean it like that. This whole thing has me on edge."

"I guess once you're considered the bad boy, the reputation sticks." His jaw tightened, holding back old resentments.

"That's not true. You're forgetting all of the people who cared about you. People like Kurt and my grandfather."

"You're right." He sighed. "I shouldn't have gone off on you. It's just been a stressful day."

"And I deserve some answers."

"Yes, you do." Although he was certain his words would not give her the peace of mind she was seeking, he owed her the truth. "I'm a key witness in a federal court case."

"A witness." She leaned forward, resting her elbows on her knees. "I take it this isn't a simple murder case."

He couldn't help but smile at the way she classified murder as a simple case. "No, this isn't about murder. It's actually a white-collar crime."

The worry lines on her face smoothed. "Well, that doesn't sound so bad."

Would it be so wrong to let her cling to the idea that this case was no big deal? Then she wouldn't have to worry. But she also might decide to let down her guard, giving that thug a chance to get near her again. No, she definitely needed to know the whole truth.

"It's a money-laundering scam that involved my business partner. I blew the whistle on him before he could take us both down. I wore a wire and gave the government all the evidence they needed to make their case against him and his shady affiliates."

Cleo's face grew ashen. "That sounds dangerous."

"Let's just say these men aren't the friendliest people to cross."

"That…that man… Does he want to—"

"Scare me off? Yes, he does. But it won't work. I will finish what I started."

"Oh, Jax. What if—"

"There are no what-ifs. I just have a few more weeks until I return to New York for the trial and then this will all be over. Now it's time to call it a night. I don't know about you, but I'm exhausted. It's been a long day."

In truth, not only was he truly tired but he also needed some space. He was still smarting over the fact that Cleo thought he might be a criminal.

Her fine brows gathered. "You can't expect me to stay here with you until the trial."

"We'll have to see how things go. But for now you're staying where I can protect you."

He yawned. Maybe tonight he'd be able to fall asleep without the endless hours of staring into the dark. Or even worse, to drift off only to have that blasted recurring nightmare where he was chased down a dark alley. Stupid dream.

"Come on." He knelt down beside her and held out his arms. "Your chariot awaits."

Cleo's head felt fuzzy. She didn't know if it was the painkillers or the information she'd just learned. Either way, it didn't matter. She was tired of being treated as if she was helpless. And she didn't need Jax making decisions for her.

When Jax reached out to her, she pushed aside his offer. "Thanks, but I can get to the bedroom on my own."

His face creased with frown lines, but he didn't argue. Instead he grabbed her crutches and held them out to her. "Are you sure?"

She nodded and placed the crutches under her arms. A bump on the head hadn't made her forget the way Jax had rejected her earlier that day. The memory still stung. Why should things change just because she got hurt?

They weren't a happy couple. They never would be.

She paused at the bottom of the long line of steps.

Suddenly, sleeping on the couch didn't sound like such a bad idea.

"Sure you haven't changed your mind?" Jax prodded in a persuasive voice.

"I can manage." All she had to do was focus. Soon she'd be upstairs and then she could lie down.

"You don't look so good."

"Thanks. You sure know how to give a girl a compliment."

"That isn't how I meant it and you know it. You're just being difficult."

He was right. But tonight she didn't care. Maybe it was the medicine or hitting her head, but she didn't feel like acting as if everything was all right when it clearly wasn't.

He followed her into a spacious bedroom with a king-size bed done up in peaches and cream. She sat down on the edge, very aware of Jax's presence. He knelt down in front of her to remove her shoe from her good leg. Why did he have to be so nice when she wanted to be angry with him?

"I can do it." She attempted to take over.

He brushed aside her hand. "You don't need to. That's what I'm here for."

His gentle tone smoothed her agitation. "I'm not even sure how I'll sleep tonight. Every time I close my eyes I see that ape man. You have to promise to be careful. He isn't a nice guy. He totally gave me the creeps."

"I'll be careful."

"You promise?"

"I do. I brought us here, didn't I? He won't know where to find us."

She lay back against the bed and closed her eyes, willing away the image of that man. Jax's warm fingers touched the bare skin of her calf, snapping her eyes open. What was he doing? Then she realized he was removing her sock. How could such a mundane task feel so amazing?

Dropping the sock, his fingers continued to work their magic, kneading and pressing on the sole of her foot. One by one her muscles relaxed and she turned to putty in his hands. The most amazing sensations coursed through her body. If he could do this massaging just one foot, she couldn't even imagine what other tricks he had up his sleeve.

"This will help you relax." His voice was soft and soothing.

She hadn't realized that she'd moaned out loud until he said, "I'm glad you're enjoying it."

"What can I say? I'm a sucker for a foot massage."

"Scoot back on the bed."

She did as he said, wondering what he was up to next. He grabbed a couple of pillows and propped up her injured leg. Then he sat down and put her other foot in his lap. The pad of his thumb rubbed up and down over the arch of her foot. She watched him as he used both hands to stretch her foot and then run both thumbs in circular patterns.

"Close your eyes," he said, still working his magic fingers.

She was in the midst of ecstasy and didn't want it to stop so she complied. Tomorrow she would stand her ground— yes, tomorrow. Tonight she would let him feel as though he were taking care of her... Just so long as his fingers kept moving.

Time slipped by and, at last, he stopped. She was lost somewhere between floating on a fluffy cloud and half-asleep. He got up and turned off the light.

"Don't go." She reached out to grab his hand. "Not yet."

"Cleo..."

All she knew was that she was in a happy place and she

didn't want it to end. Her body felt like mush. The darkness made her feel safe from his scrutinizing stare. She felt as though she could say anything to him. And in a sleepy haze she decided to throw caution to the wind.

"Why don't you find me attractive?"

She heard a swift intake of his breath. Then an awkward silence hung there.

The edge of the bed dipped as he sat down. The back of his hand glided over her cheek. "Who says I don't find you attractive?"

"When we kissed earlier, you pulled away. You didn't like it."

His voice was soft. "Did you ever think that I liked it too much?"

"Then kiss me now." He groaned but she wasn't giving up. "I've kissed you twice. You owe me."

Again there was an elongated silence. It had to be the medication because she'd never asked a man to kiss her. And it was so much easier to blame it on the painkillers than to admit how very much she wanted him. She'd never desired a man as she did Jax.

Then without warning he leaned over. His lips were just a breath away from hers. "Cleo, you don't know what you're asking of me."

"Yes, I do. I want you to kiss me. I want to know what it's like to be desired by Jax Monroe. Hope Springs's bad boy. Now a Wall Street tycoon. Kiss me, Jax. Please."

With a moan, his mouth pressed to hers. His kiss was hungry and needy. And her heart swelled. Somewhere in the haze of her mind there was a warning voice, but it was garbled and she didn't feel like heeding to caution. Here in the dark there was just the two of them.

His lips moved hungrily over hers like a starved man. And she met him kiss for kiss. Her fingers worked their way over his muscular shoulders to his neck and then her nails raked through his short hair.

The kiss went on and on and she never wanted it to end. She just floated along in the moment, enjoying having Jax so close. Because come the stark morning sun, she'd come to her senses. A relationship wasn't in the cards for her. But a fleeting moment of ecstasy was too tempting to pass up. Tomorrow would come all too quickly.

As though he could read her thoughts, he pulled back. His breathing was uneven and rapid. But as she reached out to him, he jumped to his feet.

"Cleo, you couldn't be more wrong. I want you more than I've ever wanted anyone. But this, you and me, it can't be."

"Of course it can't be," she spat out. No matter what he said, he didn't find her attractive enough. She blinked back the tears swarming in her eyes.

She'd miscalculated. Instead of the kiss making her feel better, she felt even worse knowing that he still thought that they were a mistake—that she was a mistake. She wanted to get as far away from him as she could, someplace where she could lick her wounds in private.

"I want to go home. Charlie needs me."

She rolled over onto her side, craving the company of her tabby cat. Anytime she was upset, he was right there with a loving rub and a cheerful purr. Her wounded body ached but it was nothing compared to the great big bruise on her heart.

# CHAPTER EIGHT

JAX YAWNED AGAIN. At this rate he'd need to brew another pot of coffee before lunch. He'd done nothing but toss and turn for hours last night. He'd finally dozed off sometime after three.

His mind had been crammed full with thoughts of the thug who had hurt Cleo. He'd even checked in with the police to see if the ape, as Cleo called him, had been arrested. So far, nothing. But the good news was they had his image from the resort's tapes and were working on identifying him.

Jax grabbed a spatula for the scrambled eggs. He wasn't used to cooking for anyone, but he didn't mind. What did bother him was having Cleo long for another man after he'd just got done kissing her. He snatched up a plate and placed it with a thunk on the counter.

The fact that she had Charlie in her life was for the best. A man in his position needed to keep clear of romantic entanglements. And even if his latest set of tests came back clear there was no guarantee they'd stay that way.

He drew his thoughts up short. None of it mattered because he had no intention of letting Cleo into his life—into his heart.

After the thug was arrested, Jax's plan was to return to his solitary life. With all of the money he'd made in the stock market, he could retire young. He didn't want to be one of those people who died at their desk. He wanted to get out and experience the world for as long as he had... And just as soon as this court case was over he'd get started.

No longer feeling so tired, he piled the scrambled eggs on the plate next to the buttered toast. When his friend said the housekeeper kept this place stocked, he hadn't been kidding. Jax really need not have bothered stopping at the store last night after he'd picked up the rental vehicle.

He placed the food and the orange juice on a tray, along with a red rose from the bouquet on the dining room table. Then on second thought, he returned the flower back to the vase. There was no reason to muddy the waters any further.

He carried the tray to the bedroom and tapped on the door. "Cleo, are you up?"

Silence greeted him.

He knocked louder. "Cleo, I've got your breakfast."

Still nothing.

Balancing the tray with one hand, he eased open the door and stepped inside. He came to a halt when he saw that the bed was already made up. His gaze flicked to the bathroom door. It was open and no sounds came from within.

Erring on the side of caution, he called out, "Cleo, are you decent?"

Again there was no response. He envisioned her passed out in the tub or worse. He set the tray on the end of the bed and rushed into the bathroom. The room was spacious, just like the rest of the house, but there was no sign of Cleo. He didn't understand. Where could she have gotten to?

The food long forgotten, he searched the other five bedrooms. She wasn't anywhere in the upstairs. He rushed to the sweeping staircase, which faced the wall of glass overlooking the front lawn and the drive. That was when he noticed the SUV was gone.

She'd run out on him!

But why?

Was she that upset about the kiss last night?

Did she feel guilty for cheating on Charlie?

His chest tightened. The doctor said she was supposed to be resting. What if she made her injuries worse? A knot formed in his gut. Or what if that thug caught up with her again?

He had to find her, but where did he start?

Cleo wished she hadn't been so spontaneous. Trying to get about with the aid of crutches was more work than she'd imagined. And now Jax had made her paranoid about the ape man staking out her place. She'd driven around the block three times looking for anyone or anything unusual, but nothing appeared to be out of place.

She pulled to a stop in a handicap parking space in front of her unit. She figured due to her unusual circumstances, she could park there for ten minutes—long enough to grab a few essentials and scoop up Charlie.

She'd just opened the driver's-side door when Robyn came up the walk, pushing a pink polka-dotted stroller. "Hey, girl, where have you been?"

Robyn was a good friend, but she was known for staying on top of the latest gossip in the complex. And this place was always rife with juicy stories. Cleo just hoped she wouldn't make a big deal over her injury.

Cleo reached over to the passenger seat and grabbed the crutches. With the crutches positioned outside the door, she carefully lowered herself to the ground. Her ankle pulsated with pain. It probably didn't help that she didn't take any of those pills the doctor prescribed for her. But she needed to be clearheaded for driving.

Cleo swung the door shut, almost losing her balance. She really did have to get the hang of the crutches since she was going to be on them for a while. "Sorry I didn't call again, but I didn't have my phone."

"I was hoping you were off with some hot guy, but by the looks of you, I guess that's wishful thinking. Unless you had a McSteamy doc taking care of you."

At the mention of a hot guy, her thoughts immediately went to Jax. He was definitely sexy in anyone's book. But she wasn't about to open that can of worms with Robyn, who was far too eager to help her find a "forever" guy. No matter how many times Cleo told her she wasn't interested, Robyn would still introduce her to any hot new tenants.

"Sorry. No hot doctors."

"When you called yesterday, you didn't say anything about it being this serious." Robyn frowned at her injured leg.

"I'm not that bad off." Cleo forced a smile, wanting to ease her friend's worry. "And the doctor said I was fine to go home."

It wasn't exactly a lie. She just left out the part about needing to be supervised for forty-eight hours. Come to think of it that probably meant she shouldn't be driving. But this was important.

"I don't know." Robyn gave her a hesitant stare. "You look about as appealing right now as Stephie's mashed peas. Definitely a bit green around the edges."

"Thanks. You really know how to cheer up a person," Cleo teased.

Robyn wasn't the type to mince words. And right about now, Cleo did feel pretty rotten. She hoped she never saw that ape man ever again. If it wasn't for him, she wouldn't be in this mess. The memory of him had her glancing around.

"You'll be back to normal after you get some rest." Robyn kept pace with her as they headed for their side-by-side apartments.

"You haven't seen any strangers lurking about, have you?"

"No." Robyn raised her brows. "Should I have?"

How much should she say? Probably as little as possible. Robyn had a good heart, but she had a habit of saying too much.

"There was just this creepy guy hitting on me at the casino. You know, the kind who won't take no for an answer."

Robyn's brunette bobbed hair swayed as she nodded. "Sometimes guys can be such jerks. And with you being so pretty, I'm surprised you don't get hit on more often."

"So if you see some tall guy with dark hair lurking about, call the cops."

"But what do I tell them?"

"Hmm...let's see." She stopped and thought for a moment. "I know, tell them that he's trespassing."

"Consider it done."

Luckily she lived on the first floor, saving her the task of going up and down more steps. They stopped at Cleo's door and it was then that she realized she didn't have her purse or her keys. Everything was back at the casino in her locker.

She turned to her friend. "I'm afraid I forgot my key. Would you mind letting me in?"

"Oh, sure. Let me grab the spare one. It's a good thing you gave it to me. I'll be right back."

Cleo hobbled around until she could lean against the wall. She wondered if Jax was awake yet. She'd considered telling him what she was up to, but when she'd gone to his room, the door was open and he was out cold. He was sprawled across the bed on his stomach while wearing nothing more than a pair of boxers.

He'd looked good—real good. She also remembered how he didn't want her—how he'd withdrawn from her. The memory dug at her heart.

Before turning away from his sleeping form, she'd noticed how the sheet had been pulled loose and kicked about. The pillows had been tossed off the bed as though he'd had a rough night. At least she had the satisfaction of knowing that he hadn't had a good sleep, either.

In no time, Robyn returned with the key in one hand and a baby monitor in the other. "If you lost your key during your accident, I can call the manager and have them change the lock. Of course, you know they're going to charge you for it. Like we don't already pay enough in rent."

"Thanks. But I know where it is. I just didn't have time to grab my things before they took me to the hospital." She wasn't about to add that she'd blacked out.

"Okay. But if you need anything, just phone me. By the way, Charlie wouldn't eat last night. I don't know if he's not feeling well or if he just missed you."

"I was worried about that. After his surgery, I want to keep a close eye on him. He didn't react well to the anesthesia." Cleo made her way over to the couch, where Charlie was curled up. He eyed her up but didn't make any movement. "Hey, buddy, it's okay. I'm here." She ran a hand down over his striped fur before scratching beneath his ear. Finally a faint purr started. "I'm sorry I wasn't here last night."

Instead of taking him with her, she was actually thinking of just staying home. According to Robyn there hadn't been any strangers lurking about. Apparently ape man had other people to push around.

The sound of the baby stirring came across the monitor. "I better go check on her," Robyn said, stepping out onto the walkway. "If you need anything else just let me know."

With her neighbor gone, Cleo turned to Charlie. "You do know that I'm going to be in trouble when Jax finds out I'm here with you."

Charlie blinked and licked his paw.

"I see you aren't the least bit worried. That makes one of us." She ruffled the fur on his head before locking the front door.

It was nice that Marylou had picked her out some new clothes, but they weren't really her taste and right now, she needed soft, stretchy shorts to get over her cast. And a comfy T-shirt. She may enjoy dressing up on most occasions, but this was different. Her body ached in places she didn't even think had been injured. Some loose-fitting clothes were definitely in order for today.

She hobbled toward the bedroom with Charlie leading the way. His tail hung low and he wasn't chatty like normal. The poor fellow. She felt really bad for him having surgery. At this point, she could kind of relate to not feeling so chipper. She'd have to remember to grab a bag of his favorite treats to take with them.

When her gaze landed on her bed, she thought that it never looked so inviting. So soft and snug. Maybe if she just lay down for a moment, she'd get her wind back. And she could give Charlie some much-needed attention as his love meter seemed to be low.

When Charlie eyed the bed hesitantly as though he wasn't so sure he could jump that high after his surgery, she scooped him up and deposited him in the middle of the bed. She could tell he was going to get as much babying out of this recovery as possible. And she didn't mind it a bit. She smiled as he circled once, then twice and finally sank down on the blue comforter.

After struggling to get changed into some comfy clothes, she lay down next to him, anxious to discard the crutches, which were as much a hindrance as a help. Her hand smoothed down over Charlie's back and his purr machine kicked into full gear.

"Sorry I wasn't here to take care of you last night. Some meanie sent me to the hospital."

Charlie yawned and then she yawned.

"I don't think he'll be back. Maybe we can both stay home."

She adjusted her pillow and closed her eyes for just a moment. After all, this guy was after Jax, not her. And Jax would be a lot safer if he didn't have to worry about caring for an injured woman. Especially after he made it perfectly clear that he wanted nothing to do with her. He felt an obligation toward her—nothing more.

Staying home was sounding ever-so-tempting. And with Robyn watching her back, she didn't have to worry.

"We'll be fine. Right, Charlie?"

# CHAPTER NINE

JAX KNOCKED ON the apartment door.

When there was no sound, he thought of trying the doorknob. But considering he might have mixed up Cleo's unit number, he wasn't going to risk it.

He rapped his knuckles again. Louder this time.

An adjacent door swung open and a young woman with straight brown hair, no makeup and stains on her blue shirt stuck her head out. She eyed him up suspiciously.

Maybe she'd know Cleo's whereabouts. He stepped toward her when she held up a cell phone. "Don't come any closer or I'll call the police."

"Hey, I don't want any trouble. I'm just here to see Cleo. This is her apartment, isn't it?"

"Don't play innocent with me. Cleo told me you'd be showing up and causing trouble. She's not interested in you. Time to move on, buddy."

Cleo told her neighbor about him? And what exactly had she been saying? It sure sounded bad.

Turning away from her kiss had been one of the hardest things he'd ever done. And if given another chance, he didn't know if he was strong enough to resist her.

Just then the door to Cleo's apartment opened. "Jax, how'd you get here?"

For the first time since he found her missing, he

breathed easy. His initial instinct was to pull her into his arms, but one glimpse of the wounded look in her eyes had him frozen in place. It was for the best, even if it didn't feel like it at the moment.

Giving in to his desires was what kept getting them into trouble. First they kissed and she took off only to run into ape man. And then there was last night's kiss, where she got upset and left without a word. This time he wasn't giving her another reason to walk away.

"Do you want me to get the police?" The young woman looked far too eager to place the call.

Jax rolled his eyes. "Please tell her that I'm not here to hurt you."

Cleo smiled as though she was enjoying this. He didn't find it the least bit amusing. He hadn't thought about anything besides her safety on the ride here. A tension headache spanned his forehead. He didn't know what he'd have done if she hadn't been here.

"It's okay, Robyn." Cleo smiled at her neighbor. "Jax is an old friend of mine. He's been looking after me since my accident."

The woman's whole demeanor changed and a smile pulled at her lips. "No wonder you didn't come home last night. I wouldn't have, either."

Cleo sighed. "Robyn, it's not what you're thinking."

"Then you must be blind, girl. Otherwise how could you pass him up?" Robyn flashed Jax a bright smile before backing into her apartment and closing the door.

Color flooded Cleo's cheeks, giving them a rosy glow. "I'm sorry about her. Robyn means well but is a bit misguided at times."

He nodded, understanding why Cleo wasn't eager to hook up with him the way her neighbor thought she should be. And that reason was named Charlie. Jax's jaw tightened. He at least wanted to get a look at this guy.

Cleo adjusted her crutches. "How did you get here?"

"I didn't have much choice. I took a taxi."

"Oh. Sorry. I was only borrowing the SUV. I would have brought it back."

From the looks of her in a rumpled T-shirt and mussed-up hair, he'd just awoken her from a nap. "I take it you weren't in any hurry to come back." He pressed his hands to his waist and frowned at Cleo. "Mind telling me what's so urgent that you had to go and run off without saying anything to me?"

"Charlie needed me. And...and you were sleeping. I didn't want to bother you since I figured you'd try to stop me."

"You're right. I would have." Jax's body tensed. "This Charlie, is he that important to you?"

She nodded. Just then there was a meow and Jax looked down to find a tabby cat rubbing against Cleo's ankles before stepping outside.

"Charlie, come back."

That was Charlie? Her cat? The knot in his gut eased. Then in spite of himself, he laughed. He'd been jealous over a cat.

"Don't just stand there laughing," she said. "Grab him."

Charlie appeared to be enjoying himself, exploring the great outdoors. When Jax set off in pursuit, the cat picked up speed.

"Here kitty, kitty."

"His name is Charlie."

Of course it was. He felt like such an idiot for getting bent out of shape over a cat. Not that he had any right to be jealous of anyone. On second thought, it would have been better if Charlie had turned out to be her boyfriend.

He could put her safety in another man's hands and walk away. At least he wanted to believe he could have turned his back and forgotten her.

The cat stopped to investigate a potted plant and Jax made his move, wrapping his hands around the cat's rib cage.

"Be careful," Cleo called out. "Support his back feet."

Jax adjusted his hold and the cat seemed to relax. That was good because he didn't know one thing about felines. His family didn't have cats or dogs. Not even goldfish. His father thought that they were a waste of money. That was what he'd loved about the Sinclair's ranch. They had lots of animals, from cats to steers. He'd always dreamed of living on a spread like theirs. So when the senior Sinclair took him under his wing and showed him how to work on a ranch, he was thrilled. He'd done something he enjoyed while making some pocket money.

"What are you smiling about?" Cleo eyed him. "Did Charlie find your ticklish spot?"

"Not hardly." He wasn't ticklish.

Cleo sighed. "Well, bring him inside and be gentle. He just had surgery."

Jax stared down at the furball. It didn't look as if anything was wrong with him. But Jax would take Cleo's word for it and as carefully as possible placed the cat on the couch.

"Enough about the cat. What I want to know is why you took off. Don't you realize that the thug who hurt you is still out there?"

"I was careful."

"I talked to the police on my way here." He waited to see if the reminder of their situation would gain her attention.

She didn't raise her head to look at him. Instead she

fussed over the cat. "What did they say? Has he been arrested?"

"No. And he was spotted in this area last night, but he eluded the police in the darkness."

She glanced up. The light in her eyes dimmed. "Oh. I didn't think—"

"Exactly. Now let's get you out of here."

He strode over and reached for the door.

"Wait. I'm not ready. I want to grab a few things. And you'll need to load the litter box in the car while I put Charlie in his carrier."

"I don't think so. I'm not hauling some howling cat around in the car."

Cleo frowned at him. "Charlie doesn't howl. He's not a dog."

"Howl. Meow. It's all the same." He wasn't a cat person.

"And don't forget to scoop the litter before loading it."

"No way. I'm not hauling around a litter box and a cat."

A few minutes later, Cleo settled on the passenger seat of the SUV. "Did you remember to grab extra kitty litter?"

"Yes." Jax's grumpy tone made her smile. "I don't know how something so small can require so much stuff."

He'd grow to like Charlie. She was sure of it because beneath all of that gruff, Jax had a big heart, even if he refused to acknowledge it.

"It's okay, Charlie. He's not normally this grouchy. He just woke up on the wrong side of the bed."

"I did not," Jax grumbled from the hatch as he stowed away her crutches.

In no time at all, they were on the road. She noticed how Jax kept checking the mirrors. She supposed she hadn't made the wisest choice this morning. Her gaze moved back to Charlie—but he needed her.

She glanced at Jax as he focused on traffic. "How long are you planning to keep us hidden away?"

Jax's fingers tightened on the wheel. "As long as it takes to make sure you're safe."

"I'm not your responsibility. I moved to Las Vegas to get away from my family and their overbearing expectations and overprotectiveness. Now you're trying to do the same thing."

"Well, if you don't like staying with me, I can get you an airline ticket. I'm sure your mother would enjoy the visit—"

"No!"

Jax glanced her way. She pressed her lips together, feeling stupid for reacting so strongly. If she wasn't careful Jax would start asking questions—questions she didn't want to answer. Once he knew what she'd done—the irreparable damage she was responsible for—it'd only confirm his decision that she was not worthy of his attention. She couldn't bear to have him look at her the way her mother had done.

"I can't go back there. Hope Springs is in my past."

"And does that include your family?"

She shrugged. A mix of feelings churned in her stomach, making her nauseous.

"What's going on, Cleo? Your family used to mean everything to you. Now you'll do anything to send them money, but you balk at the mention of visiting them."

His voice was soft and soothing, inviting her confidence. Still, she worried about what he'd think of her once he knew.

"Cleo, I'm concerned about you. Something serious is going on. And if you won't give me the answers then I'll have to go to Kurt for the truth—"

"No!" Her fingers twisted together. "Don't do that. I—I'll tell you."

He had her between a rock and a hard place and she hated it. Dredging up these painful memories would be torture. And for the first time to speak them out loud would just make what happened so fresh in her mind.

While living in Las Vegas, she'd been able to pretend that things were okay. To colleagues, she'd act as though she had a loving family missing her back in Wyoming. She was able to bluff her way through most days, but not today.

Maybe it would do her some good. Getting it off her chest might help. For so long now she'd been choking down the anger and hurt. She drew in a deep breath to steady her nerves.

"Things haven't been the same since my father died."

Jax cleared his throat. "Your brother mentioned that there'd been some drama at your father's funeral, but he didn't go into details and I didn't push. I figured he'd tell me if he wanted me to know."

"It was all about me." The weight of guilt settled on her chest. "The funeral was…was my fault…"

"What?" Jax pulled off the side of the deserted roadway and put the vehicle in Park. "Cleo, you aren't making any sense."

His face started to blur behind a wall of unshed tears. She blinked repeatedly. "It's my fault that my father died."

"How? Weren't you living here in Las Vegas at the time?"

"I'd just moved here." She inhaled a steadying breath. "I was on the phone with him and we were arguing. I didn't know at the time that he was in the pickup, transporting a mare he'd bought in hopes of luring me home. I might not like working around the ranch, but I still have a big soft spot for horses and he knew it."

Jax didn't say anything. He just reached out and squeezed her hand, allowing her to proceed at her own pace. This was something she'd never shared with anyone…ever.

Somehow it seemed fitting that she turned to Jax. He wasn't as close to the situation as her family and yet he wasn't so distant, either.

Cleo inhaled a steadying breath. "He kept telling me to come home. He was always going on about how much my mother missed me, but I didn't want to hear it. I was so stubborn. So determined that everything had to be my way. I was finally away from that suppressive atmosphere and making decisions for myself. I didn't want to go back and marry one of the locals. It might be the right life for some people…but not me."

The backs of her eyes smarted as a tear spilled onto her cheek. She dashed it away. This wasn't the time to fall apart. She needed to get through this. After all, Jax deserved to know what sort of woman he was putting his neck on the line to protect.

"No one can blame you—"

"But they do. And they should. If only I hadn't fought with him…he wouldn't have died."

"You don't know that." He placed a finger beneath her chin and lifted her face to meet his gaze. "And you can't live your life according to someone else's wishes. At some point you have to stand your ground."

She shook her head. "Sometimes the price is just too steep."

He gave her hand a squeeze. She drew strength from his touch.

"I—I told him—" her throat grew thick as she pushed through "—that there wasn't anything that he could say or do to get me to come home."

Another tear splashed onto her cheek. She sniffled and

ran the back of her hand over her cheeks. Why had she been so stubborn? So determined that she was right?

She pulled her hand from Jax's, no longer feeling worthy of his understanding. And he'd have no choice but to agree once she told him the price of her independence.

Her voice cracked with emotion. "Those were the last words I spoke to him."

She stared straight ahead at the desert, not wanting to see the look of disgust in Jax's eyes. She wouldn't be able to finish if she looked at him.

"The line… It went dead. I thought he'd hung up on me. I thought… Oh, it doesn't matter." She sniffled, trying to maintain a bit of composure. "I found out later…that he'd blown through a stop sign. He…he was broadsided."

Jax leaned forward, squeezing her shoulder. "It was an accident. It could have happened to anyone."

"But it didn't." She turned to Jax. "If I hadn't been arguing with him, he wouldn't have been distracted. He always obeyed stop signs. This is all on me."

"How do you know that he wasn't tired? Or he hadn't been distracted by something falling off the dashboard or the seat. Maybe he reached over to pick it up."

She shook her head, taking a second to collect herself. "I know what happened because there was an investigation. The police determined he was talking to me at the time of the accident."

"I'm sorry, Cleo. But this isn't your fault."

"My mother would disagree. She totally flipped out on me. She ordered me out of the funeral home. She said as far as she was concerned, she…she had no daughter."

"She didn't mean it—"

By now the tears were running unleashed. "Yes, she did. I was banished from Hope Springs. I tried to call a couple of times after that, but she hung up."

"She was in shock and mourning the loss of your father. I'm sure she didn't mean it."

"Even my brothers have changed. They speak to me, but it's not the same. Nothing is the same. Everyone blames me and they're right. This is my punishment."

Jax placed a finger beneath her chin and turned her head until she was facing him. "None of them had any right to lay this at your feet. You didn't know he was on the phone while driving. Not to speak ill of the dead, but the decision to talk on the phone while driving is all on him. And second, he didn't have a right to demand you come home."

Had she heard Jax correctly? Wait. This wasn't the way she thought this conversation would go.

"You don't blame me?"

"Of course not. And if your mother had been thinking clearly, she wouldn't have blamed you, either. It was an accident. And no one person was to blame. It was a culmination of events."

She wanted to believe him—wanted to shed the weight of guilt that had kept her isolated in Las Vegas through the lonely holidays, missing how her brothers would gather around the tree on Christmas Eve passing out gifts. And later how they'd argue over who got to carve the turkey.

Cleo blinked repeatedly. She might not have wanted to be a rancher, but that didn't mean she wanted to walk away from her family. She just wanted them to respect that she was grown-up now and fully capable of making her own choices on where she lived and how she lived her life. In her worst nightmare, she never dreamed she'd be labeled a black sheep and banished from her home.

"Remember when you were a kid, you always had your head in the clouds." Jax looked her in the eye. "You dreamed about those fancy fashion shows and how you wanted to travel to Milan and Paris. I never saw anyone who liked clothes as much as you."

She lifted her head to look him in the eye. "You remember that?"

"Those days that you'd sit and talk about places you'd learned about in one of your magazines taught me something important. You made me realize I could dream bigger than Hope Springs."

"I thought you were bored stiff listening to me."

"Not at all. You were like a breath of fresh air after hearing my father rant on and on about all of the injustices in this world." Jax leaned toward her. "You don't know how much I enjoyed our talks down by the creek."

"You mean when you were supposed to be fishing. And I was supposed to be quiet so as not to scare off the fish." They shared a smile.

"But you were so much more interesting." He leaned closer. "I had a hard time keeping my attention on my fishing pole. I'm lucky a big fish didn't swim off with it because you were all I could think about."

He'd noticed her? How had she missed the signs?

His fingers stroked her cheek. "But you were far too young and most definitely off-limits back then."

"And now?" Where had that question come from?

"And now I can do this…"

His hand slipped down to cup her neck. Could he feel the way he made her pulse jump? Did he know in that moment she couldn't think of anything but him?

With mere inches between them, she wondered if he'd put her out of her misery and kiss her. Her gaze moved from his tempting lips to his eyes. They were dark with a definite glint of interest in them.

Her heart pounded so loud that it was the only sound

she could hear. Logic fled her. Instead she mentally willed him closer. Her eyelids slid shut as her anticipation grew.

And then he was there. His lips tentatively pressed to hers.

Butterflies fluttered in her stomach. This was like an out-of-body experience where her body did what it desired and she sat back luxuriating in the most exquisite sensations. She didn't think it was possible but with each kiss, they got better. She wasn't sure how he could improve on perfection, but somehow he did.

She leaned into his kiss, meeting his hunger with her own. Her head spun and she didn't want this moment to end. She reached out to him, wanting to pull him closer, but the darn seat belts did their jobs and restrained them, as did the cat carrier in her lap.

Charlie meowed his protest at being jostled around. They pulled apart. But Jax's gaze held hers and she wanted to know what he was thinking—what he was feeling. But a louder protest from the cat carrier drew her attention.

She squeezed her fingers past the metal bars, trying to soothe Charlie. "It's okay, boy. I didn't mean to bounce you around."

Jax shifted the SUV into gear. "You know if it wasn't for you and your dreams, I never would have dared to imagine another life for myself. I'd have most likely given up on school and ended up just as disillusioned about life as my father. It's hard to tell where I'd be now."

She smiled through her tears. "You probably wouldn't be sitting on the side of the road with a crying woman who's holding a cat on her lap."

"Probably not. But right now, I can't think of anyplace I'd rather be."

Jax eased back onto the roadway and they headed north

to their five-star getaway. Her stomach quivered as she wondered where they went from here. Was this all some sort of sympathy? Or was there a deeper meaning to that kiss?

# CHAPTER TEN

TREAD CAREFULLY.

After a week of sharing the mansion, Jax found himself susceptible to Cleo's enchanting spell. He'd found her fascinating as a kid, and as a woman, she was near irresistible. But no matter how sweet and enticing she may be, he couldn't keep finding excuses to touch her—to kiss her. The best thing he could do was find a way to reunite her with her family.

But first, he had something he had to do. He was tired of waiting for the doctor's office to call. He could only figure they'd lost his new number and that was why they hadn't called with his test results.

He glanced around for Cleo. Not finding any signs of her, he grabbed the cell phone from the kitchen counter and dialed the familiar number. After two rings, it switched to a prerecorded message announcing the doctor was out of the office for the next week.

Jax cursed under his breath and resisted the urge to throw the phone across the room. Of all the times for the doctor to have a personal life, why did it have to be now?

The distinct sound of Cleo's crutches echoed down the hall. He cleared the number and placed the phone back on the counter. He'd just turned around when she entered the room.

She stopped in front of him with a frown marring her beautiful face. "Have you seen Charlie?"

"I wasn't exactly looking for him. Why?"

"I don't know. He's just usually wherever I am, and I haven't seen him since first thing this morning."

"In a house this size it wouldn't be hard for him to find a hiding spot."

A frown settled on her face. "I know, but I just worry."

She fussed over that cat like a mother caring for a young child. The image of her holding a baby in her arms came to mind. That was yet another reason why they shouldn't be playing house.

Jax shifted his weight from one foot to the other. "I'll... um, go look around for him. Why don't you sit down? You know what the doctor said about resting."

"How could I forget? You remind me every day." She started toward the family room before calling over her shoulder, "While you're upstairs would you mind grabbing the blue tote bag from my bedroom?"

"Your wish is my command."

He took the steps two at a time. His gaze scanned the hallway for any sign of the feline. How in the world was he going to find a little cat in this big house? He'd probably found a nice dark corner to take a catnap.

But first Jax needed to get the bag for Cleo. He worried that she was overdoing it and he didn't want her to reinjure herself. He told himself that it was no more care than he'd give to a coworker or neighbor... But then again he wouldn't be kissing them. And with each passing day it was getting harder to keep Cleo at arm's length.

Not only was he painfully attracted to her, but her passion for life made him want to set out on a new adventure. He found himself daydreaming about having a full life—no longer spending his days chained to a desk and computer. His thoughts trailed back to Hope Springs with its wide-open spaces and its endless possibilities. But most of all, he envisioned Cleo by his side.

However, for that to happen, he'd have to sentence her to an eventual life of caring for an ill man with a tenuous future—only to wind up a young widow. Cold fingers of apprehension gripped his throat, cutting off his breath. He refused to do that to Cleo. He banished the unsettling thoughts to the back of his mind. No matter how tempting a life with her might seem, he couldn't put her in that horrendous situation.

With the blue bag in hand, he returned to the family room, where Cleo had turned on the big-screen TV. A fashion design competition was on. "I take it you still enjoy clothes."

She nodded while rummaging through the oversize bag and pulling out a sketch pad and a pack of pencils.

"Some things don't change."

"Did you find Charlie?" She glanced at him expectantly.

He'd forgotten about the furball. Where in the world did he even begin to look for the cat?

As though reading his mind, Cleo said, "You'll have to get down on all fours. He likes to nap in cozy, dark spots."

Jax expelled a sigh. He might as well start in here. "Here kitty, kitty."

He crawled around on the floor looking under every piece of furniture in the room. There was no cat to be found.

Jax sat up on his knees next to Cleo. "He isn't in here." His gaze moved to the sketch pad in her hands. "What are you doing?"

She jerked the pad against her chest. "Why?"

"I'm curious."

"You'll just laugh."

"Why would I laugh? Obviously you're drawing something that's important to you. I'm just curious what it is."

Her shoulders drooped and the lines in her face eased. "It's just that when I was growing up my brothers would always poke fun at my drawings. I guess I didn't realize, until now, how touchy I've become."

"Can I see? I promise to be on my best behavior."

Her mouth pulled to the side as she thought it over before she nodded. When she turned the pad around, he sat up straighter, truly interested. There was the outline of a woman with no face, but the details were in the soft pink dress with a long skirt and a halter-style top.

"That's impressive." He meant it. "Instead of going to college to become an accountant, you should have considered pursuing art."

"You really think it's that good."

He nodded. "If I had to draw it, there'd be a stick figure on the page. It wouldn't be that good of one, either. And as for the clothes, um...do rectangles and squares count?"

"I don't think so. They'd be awfully uncomfortable."

The rays from Cleo's smile filled his chest with warmth. Until that moment he hadn't realized how empty his life had been, even before the cancer. Sure, he had his work, and his amazing success at such a young age was very rewarding. But when he returned to his apartment in the evenings, it was dark and empty. There wasn't so much as a fish or a Charlie waiting for him.

He didn't know how he'd ever go back to that solitary life after sharing this place with Cleo...and her furball. The cat really wasn't so bad after all. In fact, he rather liked the little guy, which was probably a good thing since the cat had taken to snuggling up on his chest when he was sleeping. He'd surprisingly grown used to Charlie's nightly visits.

Jax knew he was setting himself up for a fall because this arrangement was not permanent—no matter how much he might like it to be otherwise. But he had resolved not to fight it. There was no harm in enjoying Cleo's company—as long as he kept his hands to himself.

"So what do you do with your drawings?"

"Actually they are sketches of clothes I plan to make." Her eyes never left his, as though she was anxious to gauge his reaction. "Aren't you going to say anything?"

"I don't know what to say except...wow! You're a lady of many talents."

"You're really impressed?"

"Of course I am. Did you make what you're wearing now?"

His gaze moved to the pink-and-white tiny T-shirt and gray sweat shorts. It didn't matter what she wore, she always looked beautiful.

Cleo shook her head. "I only make dress clothes like the ones you saw me in at the Glamour Hotel."

"Have you been doing this for long?"

She nodded. "My grandmother taught me how to sew at an early age. She was a very patient woman. More so than I could ever hope to be."

He glanced through her sketchbook. Each drawing was more impressive than the last. "Have you sent these out to professionals?"

Color infused her cheeks. "I couldn't do that."

He caught the uncertainty in her eyes. "I'm no expert, but I think you should follow your dream. If you want I can make some calls."

"No!" She grabbed the sketch pad from him. "I already

know my clothes aren't good enough. I've been told they're too frivolous. It'd be a waste of time."

Anger warmed his veins. "And who told you that?"

"My parents. They said that if I insisted on going to college that I must take up a skill that was practical and would eventually provide me with a substantial income when I finished."

He wanted to argue with her and those misconceptions that her parents drilled into her head. They had stolen her dreams. And now he was determined to find a way to give them back to her.

Jax sat down on the carpet and leaned an elbow on the couch near Cleo's pink-painted toes. "Boy, your parents were more set in their ways than I ever imagined."

"Now you're seeing why I moved across the country for college and why I was arguing with my father…"

Not wanting her to return to that dark, quiet place where she locked him out, he said, "So this sketch, is it an outfit for yourself?"

Her gaze snapped back from that faraway look. "Um… no. It's actually for Robyn. She's always going on about my clothes and how pretty they are, which is so sweet. Anyway she wanted me to make an outfit for her. It's nice to have someone appreciate my efforts."

If Cleo ever hoped to make peace with her mother, she had to lighten up on her. Maybe he could try to help bridge that gap. He hated the thought of Cleo with no family. He wouldn't wish a solitary existence on anyone, especially when he knew as sure as he was sitting there that deep down where it counted, her mother loved her.

"Cleo, did you ever think that maybe your parents saw your fashion magazines and your high-class creations as a rejection of the life they chose to lead? Or maybe they were afraid that if they encouraged you to follow your dreams that you'd up and leave Hope Springs—leave them."

A light shone in her eyes. "But I never looked down on them or the ranch. It's my...was my home."

"But every time you complained about having to ride the fence line or feed the herd, maybe they took it as a strike against their lifestyle. I'm not saying it was right what they said or how they made you feel, but maybe they thought if you lost interest in fashion that you would realize the ranch was the right place for you."

Cleo's fine brows arched. "You really think that's what it was about?"

Jax raked his fingers through his hair. "I don't have all of the answers. I just know that a mother's love runs deep. You've both made mistakes. How long has it been since you tried to talk to her?"

"Almost two years. The last time I called was a month after the funeral. She told me never to call again." Cleo's eyes shimmered and she blinked repeatedly.

"Try to forget what she said in a moment of grief and follow your heart. When you talk to her be honest about who you are and what you want in life. Maybe she'll surprise you. What do you have to lose?"

Cleo shook her head. "I—I can't do that. I can't have her say those hurtful things again. I'm fine with the way things are now."

"Then you're lying to me and yourself. This distance isn't making you happy. You may have all of the independence in the world, but it'll never replace the love of your family. And don't doubt that they love you just as much as you love them." He got to his feet. "Now I have a cat to track down."

He didn't want to push Cleo too far too fast, but before they went their separate ways, he hoped she'd work up the

courage to call home. The sooner, the better. Otherwise
he wasn't sure if he could just walk away from her and
leave her alone.

A few days later, Cleo was still thinking over Jax's words.
The fact that he'd come to her mother's defense she found
confusing. Why was he pushing this? There had never
been any love between him and her mother. In fact, as a
kid, Jax used to revel in egging her mother on by doing
things to irritate her. So why was he suddenly coming to
her mother's aid?

It didn't make any sense. But more than that, Cleo didn't
feel worthy to be part of the Sinclair clan any longer. Not
when her actions contributed to her father's death—the
man who gave her the dream of an Ivy League school even
though he'd had to put the family's heritage at risk to do
it. And how did she repay him? By her last words to him
being ones of anger.

Cleo gave herself a mental jerk. She wasn't going down
that painful road again. She'd thought she'd tucked all of
these memories into a locked box in the back of her mind.
Now the memories had broken the padlock and were spill-
ing out faster than she could push the lid closed.

What she needed to do was quit thinking. She'd done
enough of that all afternoon and right about now, the most
delightful aroma was coming from the kitchen.

Tired of sketching, she closed the pad and placed it on
the glass coffee table alongside her colored pencils. She
grabbed the crutches that she was now more adept at using
and made her way to the kitchen.

From the hallway, she could hear Jax talking but she
couldn't make out what he was saying until she got closer.
"Don't look so down. Us guys have to stick together. I'm
sure that surgery wasn't easy."

*Surgery? Oh, having Charlie neutered.* She smiled as she listened to Jax sympathizing with the cat. He continued to talk as if Charlie understood every word he said.

"Here. Maybe this will cheer you up."

Cleo turned the corner in time to find Jax doling out some treats before turning his attention back to the stove.

"So you and Charlie are buddies now?"

Jax jerked around from where he'd been stirring a steaming pot. With the spoon still in his hand, the tomato sauce dripped all over the black-and-white floor tiles. The sheepish look reminded her of the expression her brothers would get when caught stealing one of her mother's cookies fresh from the oven.

"You heard that?"

"I did." She worked her way over to the island and pulled out a stool. "I told you Charlie would grow on you."

Jax turned away and busied himself cleaning up the mess. "There. All cleaned up." He tossed the paper towels in the trash and washed his hands. "I hope you like pasta."

"Smells delicious to me. What is it?"

"My version of Sicilian pasta." He broke up some capellini and dunked it in a pot of boiling water. "It'll be ready shortly if you want to go back to the family room. I can bring it in there."

"I'm bored with my own company. Mind if I stay and watch?"

He cocked a smile. "Is that your way of saying that I'm interesting? Or am I just the best of the worst?"

She laughed. "Hmm...I'm not going to answer on the grounds that it might incriminate me."

"I see how you are," he said teasingly as he moved to the fridge.

She wouldn't have missed this for anything in the world. As he bent over to retrieve some salad makings, she couldn't help but take in the way his faded jeans accentuated his backside. There wasn't an ounce of flab on the guy. Between his good looks and wealth, why was he still single?

"So do you do this often?"

He turned around with a head of iceberg lettuce in one hand and a large tomato in the other. "No. I rarely cook."

Then an unhappy thought came to mind. "Is that because there's a woman around to do the cooking for you?"

His gaze caught hers. "And what would you say if I told you that she cooks, cleans and folds my underwear, too?"

The thought that he'd be involved with someone hadn't even crossed her mind. An uneasy feeling stirred within her. She didn't know why she'd just assumed he was available. He was sexy and rich. He could have his choice of women.

"Before you go jumping to the wrong conclusion," Jax said, "you should know that she's my cleaning lady. She's old enough to be my mother and she's happily married."

Cleo breathed easier. "That's good because I'm never going to be the other woman. Especially when I know firsthand how much it hurts everyone involved." Then realizing she'd said too much, heat licked at her cheeks.

She glanced up, catching the slack-jawed look on Jax's face.

"I would never want you to be the other woman. If you were mine, there wouldn't be anyone else in my life but you. You'd be all I'd need."

Her gaze met his. Her heart thump-thumped in her chest. She'd only ever dreamed of someone speaking such endearing words to her.

The kitchen timer buzzed. In a blink the fairy-tale moment ended.

Jax moved around the counter. "I have to take care of

the pasta, but don't go anywhere. We aren't through with this conversation."

She watched as he drained the pasta, dribbled some olive oil on it, gave it a toss and put the lid on the pan. She thought of sneaking off while he stirred the sauce, but she was certain that he'd track her down. She might as well get this over with. Her stomach growled its agreement. Her only road to dinner was a detour through her past.

After turning down the heat and giving the sauce one final stir, Jax joined her at the counter. He settled down on the stool and faced her. "Now, what is this about you being hurt by another woman?"

"It's not worth getting into the details. Let's just say the moral of the story is I let myself fall for the wrong guy. And now I know better. So let's have dinner and forget all of this."

"Not so fast. I want to know the parts you're skipping over."

She exhaled an exasperated sigh. She hated to think about how naive she'd been. She'd never be that trusting again because putting your heart on the line was just asking to be hurt—even from those that you'd least expect.

"It was my last year in college and I'd fallen hard for this guy from my public speaking class. He was charming and charismatic. Let's just say he aced the class without breaking a sweat."

"And you fell for his charms, not knowing that he had a darker side?"

She nodded. "He was perfect. Good-looking. Talkative. Funny. Or so I thought at the time."

"What kind of things did he like to talk about?"

She shrugged. "His classes. His future plans. Football. Nothing specific."

"Did he ever care about what was important to you?"

"Not really." She stopped, not realizing until that moment that most of their conversations had revolved around him. "When I had news, he'd quickly change the subject back to him. I guess I should have seen the warning signs earlier."

"It's not your fault. You tried. He obviously didn't. So what made you see him as the jerk that he is?"

"We'd been dating for a little more than six months when I didn't feel well and came back to my dorm room early from a class to find him in bed with my roommate."

Jax clenched his hands. "If I'd been around, he wouldn't have gotten away with that."

She took comfort in hearing the protective tones in Jax's voice. "Well, I'm glad you weren't there."

Jax's brows rose in a question.

"He wasn't worth you getting into trouble. Besides, I've lived and learned, even if it was the hard way. The important part is I won't be making those same mistakes again."

"But you have to know that all men aren't like him." Jax's voice grew deep. "If you were mine, I'd never look at another woman as long as I lived."

Her gaze met his. Her heart once again went thump-thump. "Seriously? You'd really only have eyes for me?"

"You're the most beautiful woman in the world." His thumb stroked her cheek, followed her jawline and rubbed over her bottom lip. His gaze never left hers.

His touch sent her insides quivering with excitement. She was drawn to him like a butterfly to a field of poppies. Not waiting for him to make the first move, she pressed her lips to his thumb. His eyes lit up with excitement. She was enjoying this new side of herself and she didn't want this moment to end.

The tip of her tongue darted out, stroking the length of his finger. She immediately heard the swift intake of his breath. He wanted her. And she wanted him. There were no strings. No promises. Just the intrigue of finding out where this moment might lead.

Jax pulled away. "I have to get the sauce… It's getting too hot. It's bubbling over. I don't want it to…uh, burn."

He moved away and Cleo smiled to herself knowing that she'd gotten to him. This thing between them, whatever it was, was not over. Not by a long shot.

Jax kept his attention focused on the food. "You know there are good guys in this world."

"I know. You're one of them."

He shook his head. "I don't mean me. I'm not right for you. But there's someone better waiting to find you."

"I doubt it." The smiled faded from her face. "Besides, the people that you're supposed to be able to trust the most are the first ones to let you down when you really need them."

"We're not talking about jerk face anymore, are we?"

She shook her head and lowered her gaze to the floor. She couldn't help but think of her family. They were the ones she always thought she could count on—no matter what.

"I honestly think you should call you mother."

He was really pushing for a mother-daughter reunion. Buy why? Was he that anxious to get rid of her and he just couldn't bring himself to say it?

Dread filled her heart. She'd been down this road before. Her instinct was to leave and not look back. She could return to the casino and he could fly back to New York. But as much as she wanted that to happen, some ape man out there was looking for them. For now, they were stuck here together.

# CHAPTER ELEVEN

BY THE END of the week, Cleo had promised she'd call her mother if he'd just quit pestering her.

Now the moment of truth had arrived. She stared at the disposable cell phone the same way she would a rattler—one false move and she'd be in a world of regret. Whatever made her think calling home was a good idea? Oh, yes, Jax. He seemed to be full of all sorts of advice these days.

And the part she hated most was knowing he was right. She missed her family. After fighting to follow her own path in life and to be able to make her own choices, she still didn't feel complete. There was a gap in her life—her mother and brothers.

Jax's voice echoed in her mind. *Deep down she still loves you. What do you have to lose?*

Inhaling a steadying breath, Cleo picked up the phone. She didn't know if she was strong enough to do as Jax suggested, but she could do the next best thing. She dialed an old, familiar number. Her stomach quivered like a dried leaf on a blustery fall day. What if—

"Hello?"

She knew the deep timbre of the male voice. "Kurt, it's Cleo."

"Cleo?" Her oldest brother said her name as if he was

talking to a ghost. "What are you doing calling? Is something wrong?"

It was not exactly the greeting she'd been hoping for. This was nothing like the cheerful calls she'd used to make from college. But then again that was another lifetime. Things had changed irrevocably since then.

"I—I— How are things there?"

"Not so good. I've been putting off telling Mom about the mess with the bank, but I need to do it soon."

"You know Mom has no head for business. That's why Dad left you in charge. If you tell her, she'll just worry." And have one more thing to hold against Cleo.

"And if we don't come up with some money soon, there won't be a business for any of us to worry about."

Cleo worried the inside of her lip, wondering if she should mention her promotion. After her accident and now with her missing work, she didn't know if she'd still have a job when she returned. Although Jax seemed certain that her job was protected. Maybe he was right.

"I got a big promotion at work." Then in her excitement, she forgot that she hadn't told her family about her job at the casino.

"That's nice, sis. But we need more than a bump in your paycheck to cover the arrears on this loan." He sighed. "I should tell you that I've had to sell off some of the stock, including Buttercup."

Cleo gasped. She loved and missed the even-tempered mare. The backs of her eyes started to burn. It was the last gift her father had given her—no, it wasn't. There was the horse her father had bought for her as a bribe to move home. But the horse had died in the same accident that snuffed out her father's life. With that sobering thought in mind, she knew she had no right to complain about her brother's actions.

"I'm sorry, Cleo. I've had to drastically reduce the over-head."

She swiped at her eyes and sniffled. "I—I understand."

Maybe Jax was right. Maybe now was the time to be up front with her family about her choices. It was time to quit sneaking around and pretending to be the person they wanted her to be instead of showing them the real Cleo.

Taking a calming breath, she gripped the phone tightly. "Kurt, this promotion is a lot more than a bump in my check. I'm now working as a casino host."

"What?" There was a pause as though he were letting the news sink in. "You mean you wear slinky outfits and flirt with men to get them to gamble more?"

"No. I wear really nice clothes. In fact, I design and make my own clothes."

She considered mentioning that Jax was one of her clients so her brother wouldn't worry so much, but under the circumstances, she realized that it was best to keep Jax and this mess with ape man to herself. It would be safest for everyone—especially Jax. And she didn't want to jeopardize Jax's friendship with her brother, if Kurt decided to act all protective of his little sister.

Without giving her brother an opportunity to hassle her about her career choice, she hurried on. "I'll forward you some money as soon as I get paid." And now for the real reason she'd called. "How are Joe, Stephen and Cassidy?"

"They're fine. Cleo, what is it you really want to know?"

Kurt always knew when she was hedging around something. "And how's Mom doing?"

"You know, same as always. Busy with this and that. But the arthritis in her fingers is getting worse. If you're really curious to know how she's doing, you should call her."

Her chest tightened at the thought of being rejected by

her mother again. She didn't know if she could open herself up to the potential for that kind of pain.

"I—I don't think that's a good idea. I tried calling her after the funeral. She told me not to call back and hung up."

"I'm sorry, sis." He expelled a weary sigh. "Mom wasn't herself after Dad died. She was angry with everyone for a long time. Most of all I think she was angry with Dad for leaving her. She's been lost without him."

"I remember how in love they were after so many years. I always dreamed of having a marriage like theirs."

"You can still have that, if you want it."

"Listen to who's talking. You're older than me and you have yet to settle down and start a family."

"I have a lot of responsibilities. I don't have time for that stuff."

Another pang of guilt assaulted her. If she hadn't been arguing with her father that day, he wouldn't have died. Her mother wouldn't have melted down. And her brother wouldn't be devoting his every waking hour to keeping the ranch afloat. Kurt might be happily married by now with a baby on the way.

"I should go." She didn't know what else to say. There were no words to repair the damage that had been done.

"Cleo, call Mom. Enough time has passed. I think she'd want to hear from you."

After promising to think it over, Cleo disconnected the call. She still wasn't sure about calling her mother. After all, her mother was right. The tragedy of her father's death was her fault—no matter what Jax said. Why should her mother forgive her? If the roles were reversed, she didn't honestly know how she'd deal with such a profound loss.

The phone buzzed, startling her. She glanced at the screen, but didn't recognize the number.

"Jax! Jax! Phone."

She didn't know where he'd been but he entered the family room at a dead run, grabbed the phone and punched the talk button. "Yes." A pause. "Yes, it is."

He strolled out of the room.

That was strange. She thought that it was dangerous to let people have their phone number because of the GPS tracking system. So who did Jax trust enough with their location? The police? And why was his face creased with worry lines?

Jax's entire body tensed as he waited for the doctor to come on the line. He paced back and forth on the veranda. The afternoon sun was hot, but his need for privacy trumped being comfortable. He didn't normally pray, but in this instance if he had any points with God, he could use some help now.

"Jax, this is Dr. Collins. How are you doing?"

Did he mean besides the stress of knowing that his clients were up in arms because the funds in his investment accounts had been seized as evidence until this trial was over? Apart from the fact some thug attacked the woman that he…that he considered a close friend? Or aside from the fact that he was secluded in a ritzy home with a woman who could make him want her with just a look?

"I'm doing good," he lied.

"That's what I like to hear from my patients. But something tells me even if you weren't feeling like your old self yet, you wouldn't say anything. Don't push yourself too hard, too fast. And if you won't listen to me, at least listen to your body. It'll tell you what it needs."

Enough of this, he needed to know where he stood. "Doc, what did the tests reveal?"

"Nothing. That is to say there's nothing wrong with you. At this point, you are fit and healthy."

"Really?" His legs felt like jelly. He sank down on a chair. "You're absolutely positive?"

"I am. You can relax now. There's no reason you can't continue with a normal, healthy life."

Immediately Cleo's face came to mind. "But the cancer, it can come back, can't it?"

There was a distinct pause. "I won't lie to you. It can. For the next couple of years we'll keep a close eye on you. If anything develops, we'll catch it early. But I would think positive."

"Thanks, Doc."

They talked a few more minutes and Jax promised to schedule a follow-up appointment in six months. By the time he got off the phone, he was so relieved, he pumped his fists and yelled, "Yes!" like a pro football player after scoring the winning touchdown in the final seconds of the game.

This was the game of his life. After months of tests and treatments, the endless wonder and worry, he could at last relax. For the moment, he was healthy.

He let himself back in the house, eager to seek out Cleo. She was curled up again with her pencils and sketch pad. She glanced up when he entered the room.

"Is everything okay?"

"Um, yes." Had she heard him cheering? He doubted it. The house was far too big for voices to carry that far. "I actually got some good news."

"You did? That's great." She smiled and patted the spot on the couch next to her. "Come sit down. You can tell me your good news, and I need your opinion on something."

For the first time since he had found the lump under his arm, he had energy and felt as if he could run a marathon. Okay, maybe not a marathon but at least around the block.

The invitation to sit next to the most gorgeous woman

in the world was just too tempting to resist. However, he forced himself to leave a comfortable distance between them.

Charlie lifted his head from where he was sleeping on the opposite side of Cleo, eyed him up and then promptly went back to sleep. He was going to miss Charlie. Every time he opened the fridge and grabbed for the bag of lunch meat, the cat knew it and made a beeline for the kitchen so he could have some, too.

Needing a moment or two to sort out what to say to her, Jax said, "First, tell me how the conversation with your mother went."

"It didn't."

He turned to look directly at her. "What do you mean, it didn't?"

"I didn't call her."

"But I thought that's why you borrowed the phone."

She went on to tell him how she called her brother instead. Jax's body tensed as he wondered if this thing between Cleo and himself could ruin a lifetime friendship with Kurt. He hated the thought of losing yet another person from his life.

"Did you mention anything about us?" He braced himself for the answer.

"No, I didn't." Cleo's eyes filled with compassion. "I didn't feel it was my place. I know how protective Kurt can be, and I know he made you promise to stay away from me."

"You do?"

She smiled at him. "Let's just say that a little sister can have big ears when the need arises. I figure if there's ever anything to tell him about us, you'll find a way to tell him. After all, it isn't like I'm a teenager any longer."

"Maybe you're right." He desperately wanted to believe

her. But he knew he was jumping too far ahead. It wasn't as if they had a future. "And right now Kurt has enough on his mind."

Two V-shaped lines formed between her brows. "Do you think I'll get paid much for the time I was your casino host? You know, before ape man ruined things?"

"You don't have anything to worry about. I wagered a sizable fortune while I was at the Glamour. And lost quite a bit. All in all you should get a generous paycheck."

"Oh, good!" Color immediately rushed to her cheeks and she glanced away. "Sorry. I didn't mean I was excited about your loss…just that I'd have some money to send home to Kurt. He sounded defeated on the phone."

"I understand." Jax wanted to ease the worry on her face, but he still wasn't sure how to go about it without overstepping. "I'd like to help."

"You would?"

"Yes. I've been doing some thinking about this even before I heard that the Bar S was in trouble."

"We could definitely use the help." She looked up at him with a hopeful gleam. "What did you have in mind?"

He wasn't so sure how Cleo would feel about his idea. In fact, he was hesitant to bring it up. Maybe he should just go directly to Kurt with it. But then again if he couldn't get it past Cleo, he'd never get her brother to agree.

"I want to buy your grandfather's ranch."

Cleo sat back. Her eyes opened wide. "But why?"

"I'm tired of New York. I accomplished what I went there to do."

"Make yourself into a business success?"

He nodded. "Now I want to try something different."

"But I would have thought you'd be settled in New York. Won't you miss it?"

He shrugged. "Some. Certainly the coffee shop down

the street from my apartment building. They have the best bagels. But I need something more."

"What did you have in mind?"

"I thought of returning to Hope Springs. I miss the wide-open space."

"You mean to move there permanently?"

"It's one possibility. I was planning to explore the idea when the strange phone calls started. I didn't want to travel to Hope Springs and have trouble follow me there. That would just reinforce some folks' opinions that I'm still bad news."

"No one would say that."

He eyed her, knowing she was lying just to make him feel better. "Your mother might disagree."

She reached out and squeezed his arm, sending a sensation zinging through his veins and settling in his chest. He stared deep into her eyes, wanting to pull her into his arms. Since he'd talked to the doctor, he felt as though he had a new lease on life.

But before he could move, Cleo's smile morphed into a frown.

"What is it?" He'd fix it if he could. Right about now, he'd do anything for her.

"I'm just worried about my job at the casino. I can't lose it."

At least he could reassure her. "You don't have to worry. Your job will be there waiting for you as soon as you're ready."

"I don't know. I didn't complete the one task Mr. Burns gave me."

"What was that?"

"Keeping you happy."

"Oh, trust me. You've made me very happy."

"Really?"

He nodded and her eyes twinkled with mischief.

She leaned forward and in a breathy voice said, "Maybe I could make you happier."

In an instant, her lips pressed to his. His heart slammed into his ribs. Now wasn't the time for overthinking things. It was a time for decisive action. His hands slipped around her waist, pulling her closer. Every nerve ending sprang to life. He hadn't felt this free, this alive, in forever.

Cleo smelled like a field of wildflowers. He didn't know if it was her perfume or shampoo, but there was something about her that had an intoxicating effect on him.

Who'd ever think that the girl who gave him that inexperienced peck all those years ago would grow up to give such passionate kisses? Her lips moved over his in a fervent hunger. And when she moaned, it was his undoing. In that moment, it didn't matter what she'd ask of him, he'd be helpless to deny her.

Her fingers trailed up his neck. Her nails scraped against his scalp. It was the most stimulating sensation. He couldn't believe the girl whose ponytails he used to pull and who would flash him a smile lined with braces was now this red-hot siren in his arms setting his whole body on fire.

She pulled back just far enough to murmur, "Let's move this to the bedroom, where my cast won't be in the way."

It was as if she'd dumped a bucket of icy cold mountain water over his head. He…he couldn't do that, no matter how much he wanted her. He turned his head away, trying to get a grip.

"We can't." He couldn't look her in the face.

She placed her fingers under his chin and attempted to turn his head, but he resisted. He felt like a wild animal that had been caught in a trap. There was no getting away.

No pretending that he was the same Jax that he'd been all those years ago.

"You can kiss me, but you can't even look at me now." Irritation threaded through her voice. "What's the matter? Don't my kisses stack up to the other women you've known?"

He swung around and looked at her point-blank. "They aren't even in the same ballpark. Yours are so much sweeter. You're amazing."

"Then I don't understand. What's the problem? Why do you keep pulling me close only to shove me away?"

For the lack of anything better, he fell back on a cliché. "It's not you, it's me."

Cleo rolled her eyes. "You've got to do better than that. I want to know the truth."

"Can't we just forget this happened?"

"No, we can't. I want you. And you obviously want me. You owe me the truth. What's holding you back?"

There was no way out of this. He supposed he did owe her the truth, but somehow that didn't make it any easier to say.

# CHAPTER TWELVE

JAX COULDN'T BELIEVE he was about to bare his soul to Cleo.

His gut knotted as he pictured her withdrawing from him—of her looking at him differently. He didn't want to make this confession. But what choice did he have? She needed to realize here and now that they could never be more than friends.

He lifted his head to meet her questioning gaze. "I'm not the same man you used to know."

She squeezed his hand. "And I'm not a kid anymore. But I think you figured that out."

He pulled away, needing to think straight. "This isn't easy for me to say."

She reached out and gripped his thigh. "You've listened and understood my problems. Trust me to understand yours."

Realizing he needed more distance between them if he was ever going to say this, he got to his feet. If she kept touching him, he'd never get these words out.

He strode over to the wall of windows and wished he could just keep walking off into the desert—where no one knew him and no one cared about his story. He honestly never planned to have this conversation with anyone. Yet somehow when he wasn't looking, Cleo had snuck past his defenses. She'd gotten closer to him than anyone ever had in his life. And now he had to give them both a strong dose of reality.

He leveled his shoulders and turned. "I have cancer."

She fell back against the couch as though his words had physically knocked the breath out of her. "Are…are you dying?"

He shook his head. "I have Hodgkin's lymphoma. Luckily I found the lump early on. And I've since been through the treatments."

"Are you cured?"

He shook his head. "But I just found out that I'm in remission."

The fright in her eyes eased to a look of concern. He wished she would say something. Do something. Even if it was to walk away. At least then he'd know where they stood.

As the silence stretched on, his patience snapped. "Cleo, did you hear me? I have cancer."

"I heard you. I'm just wondering, with both of your parents gone, did you go through this all by yourself?"

He didn't see why any of that mattered now. "Yes, I did."

"You know if you'd called me or even Kurt, we'd have been there for you."

Her words stirred a spot in his chest. The thought that she'd even offer to stand by him through such a tough time said so much about her sweet nature. Cleo may have grown up and changed on the outside, but inside, where it counted, she was still the caring and thoughtful person he'd known all those years ago.

He drew his thoughts up short. He was letting himself get distracted. He had to be sure she understood what he was trying to tell her—that he couldn't be with her the way she wanted. That this thing between them had gone as far as he could let it go.

"I'm so sorry you felt you had to go through that all alone."

"Cleo, you aren't understanding what I'm trying to tell you."

"Yes, I am. You told me that you were very sick and you had no one there to stand by your side. But now you don't have to face the future alone. You have me. I'll be there to hold your hand. Or read you silly stories from magazines. Whatever you need."

She wanted to be there for him? Really be there. Not just with words but with action, too. His gaze blurred and he blinked rapidly. No one since his mother had ever put his needs first. He glanced away and rubbed at his eyes. Someday Cleo would make some man amazingly happy. He envied that person.

Jax cleared the lump in his throat. "You won't need to do that. My treatments are done for now. But that's no guarantee there won't be a recurrence."

There. He'd said it all. She knew now she'd be wasting her time on him. He turned his back, unable to watch her walk away.

He waited. Listening. Longing for this agonizing moment to be over. Just like when he was a kid and got caught stealing a locket for his dying mother. She always wanted one to hold pictures of the two men in her life, but his father told her it was a waste of money. Some people had looked at Jax with pity and a certain amount of resignation. Others had turned their backs on him. He hadn't cared. It was the only thing he'd been able to do for her on her deathbed and it had been worth every cruel look. Why should he think that now would be any different?

But in the next moment, he remembered how Cleo paid for the necklace. He'd been so embarrassed, he'd run off. Afterward she'd never mentioned it. And it had taken him time, but eventually he'd paid her back every single penny he owed her.

The next thing he knew Cleo's arms wrapped around him—hugging him. Her cheek pressed to his back. And he could feel the dampness through his T-shirt of what must surely be her tears. Just like all those years ago, she was there for him.

He carefully turned, trying not to knock her off-balance and reinjure her leg. He wrapped his arms around her, taking comfort in her warmth. He braced himself as she hesitantly raised her gaze until she met his.

In her eyes he found understanding. How could he have ever doubted her?

He held her to his chest and lowered his cheek to the top of her head. He stayed there in her embrace, absorbing the peace that came with her acceptance of what had happened to him. He didn't know until that moment just how much he needed her to understand—to make him feel normal.

"Thank you," he whispered into her hair.

She squeezed him tighter.

He breathed in her strength and let it settle his nerves. He didn't know that it was possible to feel even better than when he got the test results from the doctor. But right now, he felt as though he could take on the world…and win.

Jax eased back from Cleo just far enough to look into her eyes. He needed to hear it with his own ears. "You're really not put off by my cancer?"

"I think you are the most wonderful man both inside and out. No disease can change that." She followed her words with a kiss that left no doubt about what she had in mind.

Believing in her words, he gave in to his long-withheld desires. He scooped her up into his arms and carried her upstairs, leaving Charlie to finish his catnap alone.

* * *

Cleo woke up and ran her hand over an empty bed.

Her eyes sprang open. The golden rays of the setting sun mocked the fact that she was alone.

"Jax?" She glanced toward the bathroom, finding it dark and empty.

Old insecurities plagued her. Her stomach roiled. What had she done opening herself up to him? When would she ever learn?

She threw on her clothes and worked her way downstairs, unsure what reaction she'd receive. Did he regret their time together? Did he consider what they'd shared a mistake?

It was better to get this over right away than to let it drag out, no matter how much it hurt. It was as her grandfather told her as a kid. The bandage hurt less when it came off fast.

She found Jax in the kitchen—a room in which he'd spent a lot of time creating such amazing meals. Not that she had any appetite right now.

He turned to her. "Hey, sleepyhead. I wasn't sure when you were going to wake up." He put down the dish towel in his hands as his brows gathered. "What's the matter?"

"I woke up and you were gone."

He approached her. "Is that all that's bothering you? I mean, if I did something wrong—"

"No. You were amazing." Her stomach shivered as she continued to open herself up to him. "It's just that when I woke up and found you gone, I thought… Well, I didn't know what I thought."

He wrapped his arms around her waist. "I didn't mean to worry you. I couldn't sleep so I thought I'd make you something to eat."

"Really?"

"Honest. I thought you needed some rest. Otherwise I would have stayed and done more of this…"

He nuzzled her neck. Shivers cascaded down her arms as his lips moved over the sensitive part of her neck. Maybe she was crazy for letting down her guard with him, but she wanted so badly to believe that he was different from the others in her life.

She lifted his chin until her lips could claim his. She'd never ever tire of his kisses. She finally understood the age-old adage that the best things in life are worth fighting for. She'd known for years that Jax was special, but it wasn't until now that she knew exactly how special.

He pulled back and looked at her. "You know if you keep this up, I'm going to burn dinner."

"Would that be so bad?" she teased.

"Aren't you turning into a little temptress."

He moved to the stove and her gaze followed him, drinking in his good looks. There was just something so sexy about having a man cook for her. She noticed his off-white T-shirt and the way it clung to his muscular shoulders and broad chest. She smiled when she spied a few drops of his culinary creation dribbled down the front of his shirt. Still, he was the hottest cook she'd ever laid eyes on.

He paused from adding some spices to the pot on the stove. "See something that you like?"

"Most definitely." And she wasn't talking about the food.

She wanted to share her happiness with someone— she thought of her mother. She'd been so eager for Cleo to fall in love with someone from Hope Springs and now her wish would come true. Cleo reached out for the phone resting on the counter. Then paused. She clenched her fist and pulled back.

Her hand returned to her side. Even if she and her mother were speaking again, she'd never approve of this match. Not that this was anything permanent, maybe it never would be. She and Jax still had so much to figure out.

"What are you thinking about?" Jax stood next to the stove with a spoon in his hand.

"What?" It took her a moment to process what he'd said. "Oh, nothing important."

"It sure looked like it was important. One second you're smiling like the Cheshire cat and the next you're frowning. What gives?"

"Is that soup?" She inhaled the gentle tomato aroma and forced her thoughts away from her mother. "I smell bacon, don't I?"

"You're changing the subject. If this is about us making love, I want to know."

She shook her head, anxious to assure him that his lovemaking had rocked her world. "You definitely don't have a thing to worry about in that department."

"I don't?" He put down the spoon and approached her. "Are you sure?"

She pulled on his arms, lowering his face to her level. She kissed him thoroughly just to be sure not to leave any lingering doubts in his mind.

She pulled back and flashed him a big smile. "Now do you believe me?"

He smiled back and nodded. "Now I better get back to the stove before the tortellini soup burns."

"It smells delicious."

He gave the pot a stir before adding the pasta. "So have you thought any more about calling your mother?"

Well, that question had certainly come out of left field. What had he been doing, reading her thoughts? She sure hoped not.

"Um…some. But I don't know."

"I do." He sent her a reassuring look. "Time has passed since the funeral. I'm sure that she's thinking much clearer now. This is your mother. You need to give her a chance. The phone's on the counter."

"I don't know. Maybe I'll call tomorrow."

"There isn't always a tomorrow. I can tell you that I would do anything to hear my mother's voice again."

Her gaze strayed to the phone. Was he right? Should she seize the moment?

A movement out of the corner of her eye caught her attention. She jerked around to glance out the French doors leading to the veranda. The sun was setting, sending splashes of purples and pinks streaking across the sky. The breeze over the desert rushed past the palm trees, rustling the fronds. But she didn't see anything out of place.

Figuring it was probably just a bird or something, she turned back to Jax. "I promise, I will call her."

"Soon?"

"Yes, soon."

"How about tomorrow?"

"You aren't going to give up until you have an exact time, are you?"

"Maybe just the hour. It doesn't have to include the very second," he teased.

"Fine, tomorrow after lunch, I'll call. But I don't want to ruin tonight. It's a new beginning for us."

"Cleo, about that. We need to talk this over. We have to be realistic about things between us. Your life is in Las Vegas and mine is in New York—" His head snapped around to the French doors.

She knew where he was going with the conversation and she didn't like it. It was inevitable that sooner or later he'd want out of this relationship. "Jax, I think we should—"

"Shh…"

She followed his gaze to the doors. "Did you see something?"

His hands balled up and his arms tensed. "More like someone."

A shiver raced over her skin. "Do you think it's ape man?"

"I don't know. But I'm not waiting around to find out. Call the police. I'm going to investigate."

"But you can't. It's not safe."

"Close the blinds. Turn off the lights. And stay inside."

The thought of losing someone else she loved had her bottom lip quivering. She grabbed for the phone and panicked. She stared at the electronic device, willing her jumbled thoughts to settle. Her finger trembled as she punched out 911. Her heart echoed in her ears. Taking deep breaths, she forced herself to calm down long enough to answer all of the operator's questions.

Nausea rolled through her stomach, one wave after the other. She grabbed for the crutches, fumbling and knocking one to the ground. She cursed under her breath. With jerky movements, she struggled to reach it.

Should she hide? Yes, that was a good idea. Her head swung around the kitchen, looking for a hiding spot. She moved to the living room, but it was an open floor plan. But in the entranceway was a coat closet. She'd just opened the door when she heard the distant wail of a siren. Thank God they were close by.

Minutes later, Jax returned and she was never so glad to see someone as she was him. He rushed over and held her in his strong arms.

"Everything's okay now," he murmured.

After a reassuring hug, she pulled back. "Was it ape man?"

Jax nodded. "I was able to give the police a description and they're tracking him down. Hopefully this will be over soon."

"I'm not holding my breath. That guy seems to slip away at every turn."

"Everyone's luck runs out eventually. He's bound to make a mistake and they'll be waiting for him."

Her gaze met his. "I was so worried about you. You shouldn't have gone after him."

Jax shot her a reassuring smile that lit up his eyes. "You're talking to a man who fought cancer and won the first round. Chasing down a thug is nothing compared to that."

She hugged him close, knowing they still had to talk but this wasn't the time. Right now, she just wanted to appreciate what they had at this moment. The future would be here soon enough.

# CHAPTER THIRTEEN

THE TIME HAD come to keep her promise.

The following day, Cleo sat down in the family room. The cell phone sat atop the sketch pad. She reached out but then pulled back. She was making too big a deal of this. If Jax was brave enough to chase after ape man, surely she could find the courage to call her mother. After all, what was the worst that could happen?

Her mother could simply hang up. Tell her that she didn't love her. Tell her that—

Cleo halted her rambling thoughts. If she was going to fill her mind with doom and gloom, she might as well experience the reality. It couldn't be as horrible as she was imagining. Right?

After all, Jax and Kurt both thought that it was for the best. They wouldn't intentionally set her up to get hurt. But she worried that they based their opinions on wishful thinking. Drawing in a deep breath, she dialed the number. Her hands grew damp and her fingers were ice-cold. Maybe her mother wouldn't be home. Maybe she'd be out visiting—

"Hello?" The warm, easy strains of her mother's voice sounded the same as ever.

Suddenly the words Cleo had planned to say balled up in the back of her throat.

"Hello, is anyone there?"

Drawing together her scattered thoughts, Cleo swallowed hard. "Mom, it's Cleo."

She waited for the phone to be slammed down, but there was no click. In fact, there were no sounds at all. Had the connection dropped?

"Mom, are you there?"

"I'm here." Her mother's voice took on a weary tone. "I've been praying that I hadn't run you off for good. You don't know how many times I've wanted to call you."

Cleo's chest swelled with hope. Did this mean that they could bury the past and move forward? She wanted to ask but didn't want to jump ahead. Slow and steady wins the race, her grandfather used to say.

After a deep breath, Cleo asked, "Why didn't you call?"

A noticeable pause ensued.

"Because I...I wasn't sure you'd want to talk to me after what happened. I knew you were right. I'd overstepped in your life too many times. I had to give you this chance to decide if you still wanted to return to this family that isn't always perfect."

"I do," Cleo choked out past the ginormous lump lodged in her throat. "I miss you."

There was a big sigh on the other end of the phone as if her mother had been holding her breath. "You don't know how grateful I am to hear those words. I'm so ashamed of how I've treated you...of how I talked to you."

"It's okay, Mom. I understand. I deserved your anger."

"No, you didn't. Don't ever believe that. I've had a lot of time to think this over. I realize now that when you lived here, I tried to make all of your choices for you. I'm the reason you went so far away to school."

Cleo couldn't deny the truth of her mother's words. "There were other reasons for choosing the college that

I did. Like their amazing reputation. And the fact I got a partial scholarship."

"I know you're trying to make me feel better, but you don't have to. I understand what happened."

"The main thing is I miss my family and I've realized how important you all are to me."

Her mother's voice grew soft as though she was crying. "The day you were arguing with your father, it was because you didn't want to come home because I would be here." Her mother's sob ripped through the scar on Cleo's heart. "I'm the reason the family was torn apart. It was me! Not you."

"Mom, that's not true. It was me, too. I needed a chance to find out what makes me happy."

Her mother sniffled. "And did you? Find out what makes you happy?"

"I'm working on it."

"Cleo, I know that I don't have any right to ask this but could you forgive me for the way I treated you at the funeral and afterward? I can't even believe the things that came out of my mouth. I'm so ashamed that I spoke to one of my children in that manner. I'm a terrible mother."

"No, you're not. Everyone makes mistakes. Especially me. This whole nightmare is of my making. If I hadn't been so stubborn when Dad called—so certain I knew everything—"

"The accident was not your fault. And I'm so sorry that I said it was. I don't know if I'll ever forgive myself for turning my pain and anguish on you like I did." Her voice cracked and Cleo knew that her mother was crying, which brought tears to her own eyes. "I don't have any excuses except that I was out of my mind with grief. I had to be to speak to you like that."

"Mom, I love you. And I understand. A friend of mine explained it to me."

"Tell your friend that I'm deeply indebted to them."

That touched upon another sensitive subject—Jax. Maybe it would be best to wait—to put it off until things were more stable between them. But if this was to be a new beginning for them, she wanted to get things out in the open. There was no way that she could go back to pretending to be the complacent daughter.

"Mom, the friend who talked me into calling you, it was… It was Jax."

"No. Not him."

The palpable disapproval in her mother's voice caused dread to churn in Cleo's stomach. She recognized her mother's tone and whatever followed was never good news.

"Mom, he's changed—"

"Cleo, are you trying to tell me that you're involved with that man?"

Anger warmed her blood. Jax deserved a lot more respect than being call "that man." She may not have stood up for him back in Hope Springs, but she wasn't about to let him down now.

"His name is Jax. And…and yes, we're involved."

"But, Cleo, you could do so much better for yourself. The Riley boy is just down the lane. He's still single and he's taking over his father's ranch—"

"Mom, I thought you just got done saying that you regretted trying to make my decisions for me. Listen to me. I'm interested in Jax. I've been crazy about him since I was a kid."

"I know." Her mother groaned. "The whole world knew."

A smile pulled at Cleo's face, easing some of the tension. "I wasn't very good at hiding my feelings, was I?"

"Not at all. But why you had to choose him over the other boys in Hope Springs is beyond me."

Cleo accepted that her mother would never approve of her choices. There was nothing she could do to change her mother's attitude, but Cleo promised that she'd stay true to herself. Going forward, her choices would be made based on what was best for herself and not just to please someone else.

"But I don't understand," her mother continued, pulling Cleo from her thoughts. "When Jax left Hope Springs all those years ago, no one knew where he went. How did you find him?"

Obviously Kurt excelled at keeping secrets. It seemed she wasn't the only one not to know of his ongoing friendship with Jax. Instead of being upset with her brother, she was grateful to him for being such a good friend to Jax.

"It was fate, Mom. He walked into my life one day and we've been playing catch-up ever since."

Her mother let out an unimpressed "hmprf" sound.

"Mom, he's changed—"

"People don't change that much. Look where he came from. The nut doesn't fall far from the tree."

"You're wrong about Jax. He's nothing like his father. He takes after his mother. He's kind and thoughtful. I wish you'd give him a chance."

"To watch him break your heart? I don't think so."

"He won't do that."

Her mother rushed the conversation on to other subjects and since they hadn't talked in close to two years, a lot had happened in and around Hope Springs. In the end, Cleo grew quiet and listened. She wasn't going to convince her mother that Jax was a good guy and the knowledge ate at her.

Was it possible to reconcile with her mother when she was so outspoken in her objection to Jax?

"How did the conversation go?"

Cleo jerked around to see Jax entering the room. "Where did you come from?"

"I was out talking with the security guys. Now that we know that the thug is in the area, I've hired extra protection. I want him caught and I want this over."

"But will it ever be over? If you stop him, won't someone else fill his place?"

"It isn't likely. Remember the court case isn't far off now. Soon I'll be stepping on a plane to testify. Once that's done there won't be a reason for them to try to intimidate me or anyone I care about."

She looked him in the eyes. "You really believe that?"

"I do."

She relaxed. "Then let's hope he's caught soon."

"And now back to my question. How did the conversation with your mother go?"

"Not like I'd hoped." Cleo slouched against the couch and crossed her arms.

"You didn't expect miracles, did you?"

"She said that she'd made a mistake by trying to make my decisions for me. And then she turned around and tried to do the exact same thing. It was like she hadn't really heard me."

Jax pulled up a barstool next to her. "How exactly did she do this?"

"You don't want to know." And she didn't want to hurt him by repeating her mother's unkind words.

The frustration churned inside Cleo. If only she didn't have this cast, she'd go for a walk. But then again she couldn't do that, either, because crazy ape man was out there somewhere. Her body tensed.

Jax placed a reassuring hand on her leg. "Something tells me that you mentioned my name to her and that it didn't go over so well—"

"No, it didn't. Then she tried hooking me up with the guy down the road who's taking over his father's ranch. And she thinks that you can't change. She's the one who hasn't changed."

"Slow down. Take a breath." He reached for her hand and held it. "I think she's trying, but she's still your mom. And she'll always want what's best for her little girl."

"But that's just it. I'm an adult now. And she has to start trusting me to know what I want—right or wrong. I've got to learn these things for myself."

"Maybe it's best if you avoid talking about me. I won't come between you and your family."

"Speaking of which, Mom might tell Kurt about us. I didn't even think to tell her to keep it to herself."

"Don't worry about it." But by the frown lines framing Jax's face, he was worried. "I told you that I'm not going to come between you and your family and I meant it."

"Why?" She wasn't going to let him off the hook until he answered her. "This thing between us is special. It's worth fighting for."

He raked his fingers through his hair. "It isn't that easy. There's still so much we don't know about each other."

"I'm willing to learn."

"And what if you don't like everything you learn?"

"Why are you making this so difficult?" She crossed her arms and stared at him. "Are you trying to tell me you're having second thoughts about us?"

"I just want you to slow down. Don't rush things, Cleo. There's a lot to take into consideration."

"I'm not rushing. But obviously we see things differently."

"Maybe. I don't know." His face was creased with frown lines. "I came in here to tell you that I have to go to the police station. They might have a lead. I'll be back later."

This wasn't the end. It was just the beginning. With time Jax would come to terms with that. She wasn't about to let him walk out of her life again.

Cleo felt like a canary in a gilded cage. Only the saying didn't quite fit. Though she loved to sing, her voice was best not heard.

She was tired of being confined, even if it was in this luxurious mansion. She would do anything to get out. Today's follow-up appointment with the doctor sounded like a vacation. She couldn't wait to kick back and feel the sun on her face while the breeze rustled through the open car window.

During the past few days, Jax had withdrawn from her. He was hiding behind a wall of indifference and acting as though they were nothing more than friends. When he said he didn't want to rush into anything, he hadn't been kidding. So how did she get through to him? How did she convince him to take a chance on them?

Not even her drawings could hold her attention—they had no flash or flair. They were flat and boring. She tossed the pad aside. It didn't help that she had no fabric to work with or sewing machine to stitch together her ideas. She missed bringing her art to life. And as luxurious as this house was, it didn't come with the one place she liked to unwind and lose herself—her sewing room.

The simple truth was she missed her life, even as mundane as it was compared to living here like royalty.

The buzzer on the dryer went off. She glanced down at Charlie, who was curled up on her lap. His eyes opened but his head didn't move. She ran her hand over his silky smooth coat. With Jax holed up in the office at the back of the house, working on the computer, she'd decided to do some laundry.

"You've got to move, kitty." She picked up Charlie and placed him on the couch cushion. "I might as well make myself useful since I don't seem to be inspired to draw at the moment."

With the laundry room on the second floor, she headed up the steps. In no time, she had a load of Jax's clothes folded and placed neatly in a basket. The next task was figuring how to get the clothes to the bedroom. She couldn't imagine juggling a full basket while using her crutches, so she got creative. She shoved the basket along the floor with her foot. Granted it wasn't exactly the fastest approach but it did the trick.

She opened the dresser drawer to put away Jax's T-shirts when she noticed the glint of a gold chain. She'd never seen Jax wear jewelry beyond a watch, not even as a teenager. She lifted a couple of T-shirts and froze.

She blinked, but the pocket watch was still there.

*What in the world?*

Her fingers trembled as she picked it up. She moved to the bed and dropped down on it. When her grandfather had suddenly died, no one could figure out what had happened to the watch—her grandfather's pride and joy.

What did it mean that Jax had it?

She clutched the watch as the past unfolded itself in her mind. Like an old projector, the scenes of yesteryear started to come into focus. Her thoughts swept back to the last time she was with Jax in Hope Springs.

She'd been walking home from her best friend's house after doing homework. She saw Jax hightailing it from her grandfather's house. She'd rushed to catch up to him, wanting to show off her new outfit. It was the latest rage at the mall and she'd even put on some of her friend's makeup, hoping to convince him that she was not just a little kid anymore... After all, she was going to be fourteen the following week. Looking back now, she realized how foolish she'd been. But at the time, no one could tell her that an eighteen-year-old was too old for her.

So she'd stopped on the road and waited for him to catch up, but he just kept walking. No greeting. No teasing her. No nothing. She'd rushed to keep up to his long-legged pace.

When he noticed that she was going to follow him wherever he went, he stopped and looked at her. "Hey, kid, can you keep a secret?"

She'd nodded, reveling in the fact that he was going to take her into his confidence. She'd thought that it meant something special—that she was special. She hadn't been expecting the next part.

"Okay. But first pinkie swear you won't tell anyone, not even Kurt."

Once she'd given her heartfelt pledge to keep his secret, he surprised her.

"I'm leaving Hope Springs."

"When are you coming back?"

"I'm not. That's the point."

She remembered how she'd struggled to hold back the tears and failed miserably. Maybe that was why he'd broken down and kissed her...right on the cheek.

And that was the last time anyone from Hope Springs had laid eyes on him...except for her brother. She stared at the pocket watch, wondering what it meant that Jax possessed it. She knew that he did errands for her grandfather, but was there more to their relationship than mucking stalls and fixing fence lines?

She had to be sure to phrase her questions just so. She

didn't know want transpired between Jax and her grandfather so she didn't want to accuse him of anything. But then again, she needed to know the truth.

"Cleo, we've got to leave for the doctor's or we'll be late," Jax called up the steps.

She hastily put the watch back where she'd found it. They'd have plenty of time to discuss this later. Right now, she needed the doctor to assure Jax that he didn't have to watch over her any longer—that she was perfectly fine to take care of herself.

She didn't need him.

The bold lie settled front and center in her thoughts, weighing her down. The truth was she wanted him in her life so much it scared her.

When had Jax come to mean so much to her? Her thoughts rolled back in time, unable to nail down a specific moment when things had dramatically changed between them. Her feelings for him had grown and changed gradually as they spent day after day together.

And this was nothing like the schoolgirl crush she'd had on him all those years ago in Hope Springs. These feelings went far deeper and had a sharp edge when she thought of Jax leaving—and he would soon. He'd said more than once that his life wasn't here in Las Vegas.

This appointment was the beginning of the end for them. Her shoulders drooped. Once they got the all clear from the doctor, it'd be one less reason for Jax to stick around. And from the sounds of it the police were closing in on ape man. In no time at all, Jax would be on a plane for New York. And their time together would be nothing but another memory.

# CHAPTER FOURTEEN

JAX GLANCED OVER at Cleo, noticing that she'd had something on her mind during their trip into the city.

"Is everything okay?" he asked.

She smiled, but it didn't quite reach her eyes. "You heard the doctor. I'm healing up nicely."

"This isn't about the doctor's visit. Something has been bothering you since we left the house. I thought you'd be happy getting out of there for a while."

"I am." Her tone was flat.

She was lying, but why? He sure didn't understand women. Give them what they want and they are still unhappy. Maybe she was hungry. He could whip them up an early dinner and perhaps that would lighten her spirits. She always liked his cooking.

He eased the SUV onto the highway. "What sounds good for dinner?"

"Didn't you hear the doctor? I can take care of myself. You don't have to keep hovering and doing things for me."

"But why should you have to cook when I'm around and I don't mind?"

"But that's the thing, you aren't always going to be around. As you keep reminding me, your life is in New York. Not here."

He glanced in her direction, noticing her crossed arms

and the frown on her face. She'd been in an unusual mood ever since he told her that it was time to leave for her appointment. He sure wished he knew what had triggered it.

But before he could probe further, he spotted a much larger problem. A big black pickup truck was quickly gaining ground on them. Jax picked up speed as he kept glancing in the mirror at the vehicle's reinforced front bumper and the exhaust pipes trailing up each side of the cab.

The truck had been tailing them since they'd pulled out of the parking lot at the doctor's office. He did not have a good feeling about this. Not at all.

"Maybe now is the time to talk," Cleo said tentatively. "I found something earlier—"

"Can this wait?" His gaze strayed to the rearview mirror. The pickup was closing in fast.

"I think it's waited long enough."

"Hold on!"

He swerved over into the fast lane and accelerated. The pickup did the same. Definitely not a good sign.

"What are you doing?" Cleo screeched. "Have you lost your mind?"

"I think we're being followed. Our exit is just ahead."

He didn't bother with his turn signal. Instead he waited until the last moment then swerved over through the slow lane and onto the exit ramp. Horns blared. Jax kept going.

The pickup followed.

He just had to keep Cleo safe. He'd do anything for her. And in this particular moment, he didn't have time to contemplate exactly how deep that feeling went.

"Grab the phone from my pocket and call Detective Jones."

Any other time he might have gotten a cheap thrill out of Cleo fishing around in his pants pocket, but his attention was on more important matters. He had no idea what the thug behind him had in mind and he didn't want to find out.

Cleo quickly found the saved number on the phone and spoke with the detective. She disconnected the call. "He said to head for the house. He already has units in the area."

"Good."

A loud thump and they lunged forward, restrained by the safety belts. The SUV shuddered. The pickup had hit them from behind and Jax wasn't giving the creep a chance to do it again. Jax tramped on the accelerator. The SUV rapidly gained speed, putting distance between them. He sure hoped Detective Jones was right about the nearby units.

Cleo reached out and squeezed his leg. In that moment he acknowledged something that he'd been fighting for so long—he loved her. And he would do anything to keep her safe and happy.

More determined than ever to get them to safety, he turned right toward their gated community. And that was when he spotted the nail strips on the road and was able to cut the wheel and avoid them. Fortunately the truck behind them didn't have the luxury of time and hit the strips, blowing out the tires.

Jax slowed to a stop and threw the SUV in Park. He glanced out the side window in time to see the police arrest the thug.

Cleo took off her seat belt and shimmied over next to him to peer out the side window. "Is it really over?"

"Let's hope so."

Instead of throwing her arms around him and kissing him, she settled back in her seat. "It's about time."

What a strange reaction. Ever since they left for the doctor's office it was as if a wall had gone up between them. And he didn't like it. Not one little bit. But until he knew what the problem was, he couldn't fix it.

Jax entered the house smiling. It had certainly been a day for good news. First Cleo's doctor's appointment and now the police had made an arrest. At last, their problems were truly over.

"Cleo." He glanced around the living room. No sign of her.

He moved to the family room. She wasn't there, either, but he noticed her sketch pad on the coffee table and Charlie curled up on the couch. Something told him that she hadn't been gone long, because where Cleo was, Charlie wasn't far behind.

Next he checked the kitchen. It was empty, too.

"Cleo!"

When she didn't answer, he started to worry. Maybe she'd fallen. She'd been getting around with ease, but she did have a habit of pushing her limits. He took the steps two at a time.

"Cleo, where are you?"

He scanned her bedroom. Then he glanced in his room. She was sitting on the bed with her back to him.

"Hey, didn't you hear me calling you?"

She shrugged but didn't say a word.

He stepped farther into the room. "Are you okay?"

She shook her head this time. He sure wished she'd speak, it would make this so much easier. At least then he'd know what was wrong. He started around the bed and stopped in front of her. She was gazing down at something in her hands. It took him a second to recognize the familiar object in her hand.

"Cleo, listen. I can explain this."

"I always wondered what happened to this watch. It

was one of my grandfather's most treasured possessions. I just never would have guessed that he'd given it to you."

Jax sat down on the bed next to her. "Your grandfather was a very special man. I've never known anyone with a bigger heart."

She smiled. "I'm so glad you got to know that part of him."

"He took me under his wing and showed me that a man could make his own happiness. He showed me how to work hard for my money. And he taught me respect. In all of the ways that count, your grandfather was more a father to me than my biological one."

"I'm glad he was able to be there for you, especially after your mom passed on. He liked you, too. But that doesn't explain why he gave you this." She dangled the pocket watch.

Jax reached for it, but she jerked it out of his reach. He sighed. "It isn't what you're thinking."

"Really? And now you're a mind reader—"

"Obviously you think I came to have it by some under-handed way. But I didn't." He knelt down in front of her. "You've got to believe me. I wouldn't have done anything to hurt your grandfather. If it wasn't for him, I wouldn't be here today. I'd probably still be in Hope Springs, following in my father's unhappy steps."

Her brow crinkled as her lips pursed together in thought. "For him to give you this, it had to be for some really important reason because this is a family heirloom. Did you know that it belonged to my great-grandfather? It was supposed to be passed down to my father. And then to my oldest brother, Kurt. So you'll see why I'm confused about how you ended up with it."

"Your grandfather gave it to me the day I left Hope

Springs." Jax got to his feet and started to pace. "He told me to sell it when I got to where I was going."

She shook her head. "But why this? And what do you know about the money missing from his bank accounts?"

"I don't know anything about his bank accounts, but…" Jax wasn't so sure how she would take this and he hated the thought of letting her down. "He took care of my college tuition as well as my room and board. I didn't know how he arranged it and he wouldn't say. But when you were dirt-poor like I was and someone drops you a rope to pull you out of poverty, you act first and think later. Can you understand that?"

She continued to look at him. He could see the wheels in her mind spinning. But he hoped he was getting through to her. Finally she nodded. But he didn't give her a chance to say anything, he kept going. He had to make sure she believed he wouldn't hurt her family in any way. In secret, he'd always dreamed about what it would be like to be a Sinclair—to be a part of a loving, close-knit family.

"By the time my brain caught up with everything, your grandfather had passed on and all I could do was make the most of the generous gift he'd given me."

"And that explains the withdrawals from his bank accounts that no one could account for."

"I'm sorry." He felt really bad for upsetting the family. "I never meant to take away your inheritance. I was young and I hadn't thought through his generous offer. All I could envision was an escape from an unhappy life."

"Don't be." Her words shocked him. "If anyone should understand about rushing off to chase your dreams without thinking about what it took to get you there—it's me."

"Does this mean you believe me about the money and the pocket watch?" He held his breath waiting for her confirmation.

"You know, it's almost like my grandfather knew something all those years ago that we didn't have a clue about. It's like he knew someday we'd find our way together." She held up the watch. "And this is like his blessing for us."

She was being a bit dramatic, but he had to admit that he liked the idea. "You really think your grandfather would approve of you being in my arms?"

She nodded and smiled up at him.

Jax stood and drew her up into his embrace. He never ever wanted to let her go. She fit so perfectly against him. It was as though she'd been made just for him.

She pulled back and looked into his eyes. "What did you come in here to tell me?"

"That's right. I have good news." He paused, thinking about kissing her now and saving the talking for later. "But it can wait."

He leaned forward, but she pressed a hand to his chest. "It can't wait. I need to know what's happening."

Jax tightened his hold on her, not wanting the moment to end, but realized he might as well get this out of the way. "Okay. Apparently ape man wasn't a hired thug. He's actually the brother of my former partner. He was a one-man team out to protect the goose that laid his golden egg. Now that he's been arrested, we don't have to worry."

"Are you certain?"

"Positive. He confessed."

Cleo threw her arms around Jax and hugged him tight. But instead of following it up with the kiss he'd been anticipating, she pulled back and gave him a serious look.

"What does this mean?"

He brushed a strand of hair from her cheek. "As tempting as it is to stay, we can't go on living here forever. Eventually my friend will want his house back."

"I suppose you're right. Even if it's the fanciest house I've ever been in. Do we have to leave now?"

Jax shook his head. There was absolutely no other place he wanted to be. "I think we can stay another night."

"Good." She snuggled closer to him. "I'm just so glad you're safe."

"How glad?" He smiled and glanced at her very kiss-able lips.

In the next moment, her mouth pressed to his. She was bold and persuasive, leaving no doubt of what she had on her mind. And he liked it. He liked it a whole lot.

He met her move for move, needing to feel their close-ness once more. As she opened up to him, she tasted of chocolate. It had never tasted so good. A moan grew deep in his throat.

Things were about to change for them. They could move forward—think about the future. And the past could fall away behind them. They could make their own memories starting with today.

Because with Cleo, he was alive. She cared about him as no one else ever had. The knowledge sealed the hole in his heart—the empty spot where the love of a family was supposed to be. Cleo was all of the family he'd ever need.

## CHAPTER FIFTEEN

"Jax, you missed my street."

He glanced in the rearview mirror as the street sign faded into the distance. He'd been distracted by the way her hand rested on his leg. "Sorry. I'll turn around."

"No need. You can just circle the block." There was a slight pause. "It's great to be going home. Don't get me wrong. Staying in a movie star's mansion was an experience I'll never forget. It sure is a long way from Hope Springs, Wyoming."

"Is that good or bad?"

"Part of me misses Hope Springs, but another part doesn't want to be stuck in that small town for the rest of my life. There are so many places to see and things to do."

"You know, your fashion designs could be the key to having the best of both worlds."

"You think so?" He nodded and she continued, "But I haven't even shown anyone my drawings."

This was his moment to confess what he'd been up to while she'd been drawing. He just hoped she approved. If not, this might very well be the last time she talked to him and that thought knotted his gut.

"Actually I've been told by an expert that you have amazing talent and a bright future, if you pursue it."

"What? But how?" There was a pause as though she was trying to make sense of things. "Jax, what did you do?"

He pulled into a parking spot, put the SUV in Park and turned off the engine. He rubbed his head, suddenly in doubt of his actions, which was so unlike him. He was a man of decision—split-second decisions. That was how he'd been able to amass a fortune.

But when it came to Cleo, he felt constantly off-kilter. But surely she'd be happy about this, right? No point in delaying the inevitable.

"I sent some of your sketches to a friend of a friend. And I included a picture of you in that yellow outfit you had on at the casino."

"You didn't?" She looked at him as though she was waiting for him to say he was joking.

"Cleo, I'm serious. I sent your stuff to an industry professional. He is interested in meeting with you."

"Why didn't you ask me first?"

"I thought about it, but I didn't know how it'd work out. I mean, I'm no judge of fashion. I just know what I like—"

"So if this expert didn't like what they saw, you didn't want to hurt me."

He nodded, relieved that she understood his motive. "Exactly. I have his name and number written down." Jax reached into his pocket and withdrew the slip of paper. "He's expecting your call."

"I should be upset with you for going behind my back, but I'm grateful. Thank you. You're the first person since my grandmother to believe I could make my dreams come true without just settling for what is expected of me."

He reached out for her hand and took it in his own. "You can do whatever you set your mind to. And I'm going to enjoy watching you succeed."

She leaned over and hugged him. His heart pounded

beneath her cheek. What had he ever done to be lucky enough to have someone so special in his life?

Cleo lifted her head and looked at him. "But next time you have a brilliant idea, talk to me first. Agreed?"

He expelled a pent-up breath. "Agreed."

"Now let's get inside. Charlie is anxious to get out of this carrier."

Jax dashed out the door and strode around the front of the vehicle to assist her. "Would you mind taking Charlie while I grab my crutches? We can come back out later for the rest of our stuff. Not that there's a lot of it."

He did as she asked and escorted her up the walk. Cleo smiled and greeted the other people coming and going. This place was crawling with young people, from college students to young mothers with strollers. He could imagine Cleo fitting in well here.

"I've never had a houseguest before." Cleo sent him a hesitant glance. "You'll be my first. I wish I'd known you were staying. I'd have cleaned up some."

Staying? Here? With her? Like an honest-to-goodness couple? The reality of the situation was setting in and all of the uncertainties in the back of his mind came rushing forth—from the potential for his cancer to return to her mother's dislike of him. Jax shoved the doubts away. After all, this was what he wanted—Cleo in his life.

"I'm sure you don't have to worry." He sent her a reassuring smile even though he was feeling anything but assured. "Remember I was already here and the place looked great."

Before they could say much else, Robyn exited her apartment. She was pushing a pink baby stroller in their direction.

"Oh, look! Robyn has her daughter all dressed up in an outfit I made her." Cleo picked up her pace on the crutches.

"Welcome home." The young woman's face lit up with a broad smile. "Stephie is wide-awake and anxious for Auntie Cleo to visit with her."

Cleo stopped and leaned over the stroller. "Hey, cutie, aren't you adorable."

Jax had never seen Cleo with a baby. Her whole demeanor changed. She almost glowed as she oohed and ahhed over the child. What was it about babies that could affect women of all ages so deeply?

Jax stood back as the women went on and on about the baby. He tried his best to act as if nothing was bothering him, but inside their words were shattering the dreams he'd had about his future—a future with Cleo. With each laugh and smile, his hopes were splintering into shards that cut deep.

What made him think Cleo would fit into his predetermined world?

She was still so young and full of possibilities. His life choices had been drastically narrowed when he'd received his cancer diagnosis. Having a family of his own was not an option for him.

Aside from the question of the lifesaving treatments causing fertility issues, he wouldn't subject his child to the uncertainty of his cancer making a recurrence. He knew the agony of being a child and losing a parent. He didn't want to pass on that unhappy legacy.

Cleo had him thinking about all sorts of things he'd never thought about before. Like moving to Las Vegas instead of Hope Springs. He'd let himself get caught up in the moment. First the doctor called with the news that his test results were good and then he'd given in to his desires. It'd been like the fall of dominoes—one thing leading to another. And now Cleo was expecting him to make her happy and as much as he wanted to do just that, he couldn't.

The truth of the matter was he lived a life of uncertainty. It was bad enough that he had to live every day with a big question mark over his head. It wasn't fair to ask Cleo to give up her chance to be a mother to live with a man who could become sick again.

The best thing he could do for Cleo was walk away. Forget his dreams of making a future with her. He'd never felt so awful about a decision as he did now. How was he supposed to walk away from the woman whose smile could light up his whole world? He couldn't even imagine his life without her in it. But it wasn't as if he had a choice. He had to do what was best for her.

And that wasn't him.

He carried her belongings into the apartment and Cleo followed him. When she closed the front door, the walls seemed to close in on him. He didn't belong here. He didn't belong with her.

She proceeded to give him the grand tour of her two-bedroom apartment. "And this is my sewing room. Don't mind the mess. I've been working on an order for Robyn. Her older sister is pregnant and she wanted me to make some clothes and stitch up a comforter like I'd done for Stephie."

His gaze took in the array of baby blue, yellow and green fabrics. The knife of guilt stabbed at him for even considering asking Cleo to spend her life with him. And when she held up little bib overalls and her face scrunched up into a huge smile as if she was imagining her own baby someday in the outfit, he couldn't breathe.

He needed to leave. He needed space. Someplace where the pain wasn't so severe. Where there weren't reminders of everything he'd never have.

"I've got to go." He started for the door.

"Leave? Where are you going? I thought you'd stay here until your flight to New York."

"I—I can't."

"What's wrong? You've been acting strange ever since we got here."

He wanted to walk away without her hating him. The thought of her looking at him with loathing in her eyes made his stomach roil. There had to be a way to part on good terms. After all, soon he'd return to New York.

Maybe that was the answer. He could remind her that they led separate lives miles from each other. In no time, she'd get on with her life. She'd forget him. With her beauty, she could have any guy she set her heart on.

"I'm just tired." He could feel her staring at him, trying to guess if he was telling the whole truth or not. "I thought I'd go back to the casino and make sure things are squared away there."

"The casino?" A frown pulled at her face. "Are you tired of me?"

The sadness in her eyes cracked his resolve. "Of course not. I just… We can't pretend that my life is here. I belong in New York. I have the court case coming up. I can't back out now. Too much is at stake."

Her eyes shimmered. "This thing that happened between us. Are you saying it was all a lie?"

He shook his head. "It was a beautiful dream. One I will always treasure."

"Then why?" Her voice cracked with emotion. "Why are you doing this?"

"Because it isn't fair to you." The truth came tumbling out. "I can't tie you down to a life with a cancer patient."

"But you're cured. You said your tests were clear."

"But if it spread once there's no reason to think that it

might not recur. And I can't put you through that. Living with this uncertainty is horrible."

"But we can lean on each other. We can get through it together."

She had an answer for everything. But he had something she couldn't fix.

"And I can't give you children."

"I don't want kids." She said it way too fast—like a needy child desperate to say anything to get what they wanted without thinking of the ramification of their words.

"Your lips say one thing but your body says something else. I watched you just moments ago with that baby. I never saw that peaceful look on your face before. You were in your element. You practically glowed."

"But…but—"

"There's no but for this. I've tried to do this as nice as I could but you won't let go. Cleo, your mother was right. I'm not the man for you. I take what I want and I wanted you."

"Because you love me."

He stilled himself, holding back the rush of emotions. He'd never lied to her, ever—until now. But it was necessary. It was for her own good. But when he searched for the words to deny his love for her, his voice failed him.

She stepped up to him and stabbed him in the chest. "You can't deny it because it's true. We've shared so much. We're building something. We…we're falling in love."

"This is all my fault. I'm selfish and an uncaring jerk."

"That's not true."

"Yes, it is, or I wouldn't be putting you through this."

In that particular moment, he hated himself for hurting her. He wasn't deserving of her love.

He dipped his head and planted a quick kiss to her cheek. "Have a good life. You deserve the best."

He turned and started walking. He had to get away before she wore through the last of his resistance. She had no idea how hard it was to act as if he didn't care about her when his heart thumped out her name with every beat.

It was only after he was headed down the sidewalk to the SUV that he realized they'd done this scene once before…long ago when he left Hope Springs. Back then he was walking away from one of his dearest friends. This time he was walking away from the woman who held his heart in her hands.

# CHAPTER SIXTEEN

UNABLE TO SLEEP since Jax walked out the door, Cleo found herself spending all of her time in her sewing room. It was where she lost herself when the world turned dark and gray. And thanks to her sketch pad, she had plenty of creations to keep her hands busy. But her mind kept stumbling back to Jax.

She wanted to yell at him and tell him that he didn't know what she was thinking, but the truth was he had been pretty accurate. She'd blurted out that she didn't want kids in desperation to keep him from leaving.

It pained her to admit it, but she was doing exactly what she promised herself she wouldn't do. She was making a monumental decision based on what Jax wanted—not what she wanted. And that was a recipe for disaster.

Jax had been right to turn down her plea. She didn't know how she felt about kids. In all honesty, she hadn't given the subject much thought. At this point in her life, she still had lots of time to start a family—if she chose to.

She found herself in Robyn's living room to drop off the baby items Robyn had ordered for her sister's upcoming baby shower and yet somehow Cleo had ended up staying for a chat. While she waited for her friend to return with the coffee, she pulled her grandfather's pocket watch from her pocket. Her thumb rubbed over the engraved design.

She'd found the watch in her duffel bag she'd brought back from the mansion. She knew for certain she hadn't placed it in there because she'd given it back to Jax. Obviously her grandfather had loved Jax and wanted him to have the watch. The fact that Jax still had it and hadn't sold it as her grandfather had given him liberty to do was a tribute to Jax's feelings for him.

No man who was selfish and uncaring would carry around a memento and then hand it over to her because he saw how much it meant to her. Only a man with a heart of gold would be that thoughtful and generous.

"What's that in your hand?" Robyn asked as she placed a cup of steaming coffee in front of her.

"It belongs to Jax. He forgot it."

"He'll be missing it. You should catch up to him before he heads to the airport."

"Maybe." But she still had something to get straight in her mind before she faced Jax. "How did you know if you wanted kids?"

"That's easy. I always enjoyed them. And Mike comes from a big family. So we agreed to have at least two babies. Why?"

She could feel her friend's intent stare while Cleo concentrated on stirring the sweetener into her coffee. "The strange thing is I've never really thought about kids... until now."

"Are you pregnant?"

Cleo's head jerked up so she could gauge the look on her friend's face. She was serious. Cleo inwardly groaned. Maybe agreeing to stay and talk wasn't the best choice. She already had enough problems on her mind.

"No. I'm not pregnant. And don't even think of wishing it on me. You've got the mommy genes. The jury is still out for me."

Robyn held up her hands all innocentlike. "Sorry, I jumped to the wrong conclusion."

"Stephie's adorable, but I'm not ready for that kind of commitment. Is that bad? I mean, I'm only twenty-five. If I don't want kids now, do you think I'll never want them?"

Robyn shrugged and sat back in her chair. "I pretty much knew what I wanted early in life, but everyone is different. Do you have to know now? Does this have something to do with Mr. Tall, Dark and Dreamy?"

"He has reason to think he can't have kids and he doesn't think it's fair to tie me down. He thinks that eventually I'll want them."

"He could be right."

"Or he could be wrong." Cleo sent her friend a pointed stare.

She didn't want Robyn siding with Jax. She wanted her friend to say his logic was flawed. Because deep inside, her gut was screaming that they belonged together...no matter how her mother felt. And she certainly wasn't going to let the worry of cancer dictate her future. Life didn't come with guarantees. If only she could convince Jax of that.

Robyn shrugged and sipped at her coffee. "You said he couldn't have children. You know that's different than him not wanting children. Does he want children?"

"I—I don't know. We never really discussed it."

"If it's a matter of him not being able to father a baby, you must realize that in this day and age you have so many options to choose from."

"You're right." Hope bloomed in her chest. "I wish I'd thought of that before."

Cleo honestly didn't know if he was interested in having children or not. She'd been so caught off guard by his abrupt turnaround regarding their relationship that her mind hadn't been able to string two thoughts together much less ask intelligent questions. But Robyn had brought up a valid point and Cleo wasn't about to let him off the hook until he gave her an honest answer.

She refused to stand by and let him make a unilateral decision about their relationship. He needed to hear her thoughts on the matter. And there was no time to waste. If she had to follow him all the way to New York, she'd do it. This was too important to let the moment slip by. If there was even the slightest possibility they could make this relationship work, she wanted that chance—they deserved it. And she wouldn't be dissuaded by a truckload of what-ifs.

"I've got to go. I have a pocket watch to return." With the aid of her crutches, she stood. "Thanks for the coffee."

"I wish I could see this." Robyn let out an exaggerated sigh. "I miss all of the good parts. Just promise me you'll fill me in on the details later."

"Maybe."

While Robyn sputtered and spurted over her noncommittal answer, Cleo rushed out the door. There were some things that didn't need to be shared even with her closest friend. She just hoped there would be some special memories created today.

With a quick change into a red-and-white-flowered sundress, she felt more feminine and confident. Nothing like a beautiful outfit to bolster one's nerves. She tramped the gas as she zipped across town to the Glamour Hotel and Casino. She just hoped she was in time. She knew that Jax had booked his flight for home today, but she had no idea when it would depart. If she had to, she'd track him down at the airport and buy a plane ticket if that's what it took. They weren't finished talking. Not by a long shot.

She hustled up to his bungalow. Ignoring the Do Not Disturb sign, she knocked. When he didn't answer right away, she pounded harder on the door.

The door swung open. "What's all the racket about?"

Jax stood in the doorway. His hair was rumpled. His torso was bare, revealing his rock-solid abs. And his khaki shorts were wrinkled and hung low as if he hadn't been eating. She didn't have to ask. She could see he wasn't any happier with this separation than she was.

She drew her gaze back to his unshaven face. "You've had your say, now I'm going to have mine."

"Don't, Cleo. Everything has been said." He started to shut the door in her face.

She moved quickly, angling her crutch in the way. "What gives you the right to speak for me? And to make up my mind for me?"

She pushed him aside and entered the bungalow, which looked as if it hadn't been visited by housekeeping in days. Clothes were strewn about. Pillows and blankets littered the couch. And through all of the mess, she didn't see any signs of food. This whole mess was so unlike the clean-up-after-himself Jax who she'd been living with for the past month.

She turned to him, finding that he'd closed the door, giving them some privacy. "I've had time to think things over and you're wrong."

His brows drew together into a dark line. "I'm not wrong. You just want to believe the impossible."

"What's impossible? Us being together?" When he nodded, she rushed on, "I disagree."

He sighed and rubbed the back of his neck. "Cleo, you're just making this harder on both of us."

"Good. It should be hard to walk away from someone you care about, especially when you're doing it for all of the wrong reasons."

"I'm doing what is best for you."

"But see, I don't want you deciding what's best for me.

I already went through that back in Hope Springs. It was why I left. And now you're trying to do the same thing. It's time people listen to me and respect my feelings."

"I've always respected you and your feelings."

At last, she felt as though she was making some progress. "Then it's time you stop talking and listen to what I have to say."

"Can I at least put on a shirt?"

She nodded. But that was all she was going to wait around for. This needed to be said before she burst. Because she wasn't going anywhere until he heard her out about everything. Including the part she'd been too afraid to come straight out and say before now—she loved him.

Jax needed a moment to gather his thoughts.

In reality, he needed to back away before he pulled Cleo into his arms and kissed her into silence. Secretly he'd been wishing she'd show up, but logic told him that this talk would not end happily—for either of them. Why couldn't she have just left things alone?

He walked over to the couch and grabbed his discarded T-shirt. He'd spent the past couple of days doing nothing but trying to forget the fun and the laughter when he was around Cleo. She was his sunshine and without her, life was like a blustery gray day. But he couldn't be greedy. Her happiness was more important to him. He'd forgotten that for a moment, but he wouldn't forget it again. He just had to make her understand that she was setting her sights on the wrong man...no matter how touched he was that she chose him.

Taking a deep breath in and slowly blowing it out, he turned. "Okay, I'm listening. But I don't have long. I have some packing to do before I head to the airport."

Cleo's gaze slowly surveyed the room before cocking an eyebrow at him.

"Like I said, I have things to do before heading to the airport." He wasn't about to admit to her that he'd been so miserable since he walked away from her that he hadn't wanted to be disturbed by anyone, including housekeeping.

"Then you won't want to forget to pack this." She withdrew the pocket watch from her purse and placed it in his hand, wrapping his fingers around it.

"I can't take this. It belonged to your grandfather."

"And he wanted you to have it. He wouldn't have gone out of his way to help you if you hadn't come to mean a great deal to him. His son was busy with his own family. And my grandmother was gone. I was too young then to understand how lonely he must have been. So you filled in that gaping hole and I'm sure he took great pleasure in being able to help you."

Jax's throat tightened as his hand lowered. He couldn't believe how Cleo was able to be so positive when it would be so easy for her to hate him for taking what would have been her inheritance money and the pocket watch.

He wasn't going to continue to argue about it. "I'll keep it until you or Kurt have children of your own and then you can have it for them."

"Speaking of children, since when do you get to dictate whether I'll have any or not?"

He inwardly groaned. She had a stubborn glint in her eyes. She wasn't going to leave until he convinced her that walking away was the best option. Why did Cleo always have to do things the hard way?

"I saw you the other day with that baby. It was obvious that you're a natural mother. And don't even try to tell me again that you don't want children just because you know that I can't give you any."

She pressed her hands to her hips. "You're right, that was wrong of me."

At last, he was getting through to her. He wanted to be happy for her that she was seeing reason and was no longer willing to throw her life away on him, but it only made him sadder.

She tilted her chin. "The thing is I don't know if I want to have children. As of today, I don't. But tomorrow, who knows. When my biological clock starts to tick, I might totally change my mind."

"Then you accept that we can't be together."

"The thing is I've heard you say that you can't have children, but you've never said whether you want them or not."

"What does that matter?"

She smiled as though she knew something he didn't. "I had to be reminded that being a parent isn't a matter of DNA. And there are so many options open to people wanting to give love to a child, from adoption to foster parenting. And if we want a baby, there are sperm banks."

He was surprised by how much thought she'd put into this after her emotional response the other night. This time he was persuaded to believe she'd really thought this over. She deserved an honest answer.

"Until I spent time with you, I hadn't given kids any thought. My childhood wasn't the happiest so I wasn't inclined to be a family man, but being around you has me rethinking my stance."

"So then kids are a possibility for you, too." She smiled up at him as if she'd bested him.

"You're forgetting one big thing. The cancer. My life is lived one test result to the next."

"Then maybe you should broaden your horizons and quit living test to test. No one says you have to."

"But you don't understand, it could come back."

"And it might not. It's kinda like looking at a glass of water. You can either view it as a glass half-full or half-empty. I choose to look at it as half-full."

He raked his fingers through his hair. "It isn't fair to put a wife and child through the uncertainty."

"So you're saying that my father shouldn't have married my mother and that my brothers and I were a big mistake."

"Of course not. That's not the same thing."

"Why isn't it? My father died young. My younger brothers were still in school. We all still needed him." She stepped up to Jax and looked him in the eyes. "Life doesn't come with guarantees."

"But—"

She pressed her fingers to his lips. "I'd rather live a month or a year with you in my life than fifty years alone. You've been in my heart since I was a teenager."

He took her hand in his. "But your mother…"

"Will have to get used to the idea that you and I belong together."

"And you're absolutely certain that you want me, flaws and all."

Her eyes lit up and she nodded vigorously. "I'm absolutely certain. But I do have one question."

His chest tightened. He wasn't sure he was ready for any more proclamations. His mind was still trying to process everything she'd said. "What is it?"

"I love you. And I need to know if you feel the same for me."

Now this part was easy.

He'd been so busy trying to hide his feelings from both of them that he just now realized he'd never spoken the words of his heart.

He wrapped one arm around her waist and pulled her close. With his other hand, he brushed back her hair and looked into her mesmerizing green eyes—eyes he could see his whole future in.

"I can't honestly tell you when I first started to fall in love with you. There are too many moments to choose from. But I've been having a heck of a time trying to figure out how to go on without you."

"And now you won't have to."

"You're certain this is what you want—that I am what you want?"

"Most definitely."

He lifted her into his arms and pressed his lips to hers. He couldn't imagine how he'd ever gotten lucky enough to have this ray of sunshine in his life, but he planned to do everything he could so she never ever regretted her decision.

# EPILOGUE

*One year later...*

JAX WAS CERTAIN he'd never tire of staring at his beautiful wife. He was so glad that she hadn't given up on him and had made him see things her way—the way they should be. Together.

Cleo sent him a hesitant look. "Are you sure about this?"

He nodded and smiled, hoping to ease her worries. Over the past year they'd learned to rely on each other during moments of uncertainty. And in return, she'd gotten him to appreciate each day and to stop fretting about tomorrow. Whatever came their way, they'd face together.

"Don't worry. Everything will be fine." He pulled on a blue T-shirt. "Your mother loves you and she'll want whatever will make you the happiest. After all, Kurt finally came around to the idea of us as a couple."

She smiled at him, filling his chest with a warm, familiar sensation. "I can't believe you convinced him to be your best man."

"You do know I had to swear on my life to keep you happy, don't you?"

She leaned over to him, her lips almost touching his. The breath in his throat hitched. It didn't matter how many times she kissed him, it would never lose its excitement.

Her mouth pressed to his and he pulled her close, but all too soon she was backing away.

"Now, was making that promise to my brother such a hardship?"

"Um…not when you put it that way." He grinned at her. "Now why don't you come back over here?"

"I have to get ready." Cleo struggled to fasten her necklace. "I just don't understand why we have to tell my mother about our plans. Can't we just tell her we're going on vacation?"

"Because we're all working on building a strong, open relationship." He stepped up and helped her with the clasp. "After all, she loves you enough to give me a chance, right?"

With a shrug, Cleo said, "I guess."

"Then you need to give her a chance and be honest with her."

Cleo rushed into the walk-in closet of their newly built house in Hope Springs. She returned with a pair of blue stilettos.

He eyed them up suspiciously. Obviously his wife was far more nervous about this talk with her mother than he'd originally thought. "Um, are you sure you want to wear those to the Jubilee?"

She frowned at him before rushing back into the closet. He smiled to himself. Life with Cleo was never boring.

After he'd testified in the money-laundering case, he was hailed as a star by both the press and her family. He'd finished up his work in New York City and returned to Cleo in Las Vegas just as he promised. But after a while they agreed that Vegas didn't feel like home to either of them. So Cleo tendered her resignation at the Glamour and they bought her grandfather's ranch from the family, and in the process, they'd put the Sinclair ranch back on solid financial ground.

Cleo slipped on a pair of colorful cowboy boots. "I just don't think Mom's going to be happy with our decision. She's been hinting about grandkids since you and I said 'I do' on Valentine's Day."

"And she's just going to have to understand that my wife has dreams to fulfill. By the way, I have our tickets to New York in my jacket pocket. We take off tonight after the festivities."

"You mean after we tell my mother that we're going to put off adoption and launch a fashion line instead."

"Exactly."

Just then Charlie strolled into the room and rubbed over Jax's legs. "Hey, boy, where have you been all morning?"

Charlie meowed in response and Jax couldn't resist kneeling down to scratch behind the cat's ear. "And don't worry. While we're gone, you're going to the ranch house to visit with your other feline friends."

"Mom really has become quite the cat lady." Cleo ran her fingers over her hair, trying to improve on perfection. At least that's how she looked in his book.

"It's good for her. Now she has furbabies to fuss over instead of you and your brothers."

"If only it was that easy. I still don't think she's going to take the news well."

Jax approached his wife and wrapped his arms around her waist, pulling her close. "I insist you quit worrying. Where's that fiery woman who told me what was up when I was foolish enough to try to walk away from the best thing that ever happened to me?"

"She's still here." Cleo smiled up at him before planting a stirring kiss on his lips. "And look how wonderful that has turned out."

"And if you keep kissing me like that we are going to be quite late for the Jubilee."

"You shouldn't tease me," she taunted.

"Who's teasing?" He tumbled her onto the bed.

She gazed up at him with happiness reflected in her eyes. "I love you, Mr. Monroe."

"And I will always love you."

\* \* \* \* \*

# *Mills & Boon® Hardback*

## *July 2014*

## ROMANCE

| | |
|---|---|
| Christakis's Rebellious Wife | Lynne Graham |
| At No Man's Command | Melanie Milburne |
| Carrying the Sheikh's Heir | Lynn Raye Harris |
| Bound by the Italian's Contract | Janette Kenny |
| Dante's Unexpected Legacy | Catherine George |
| A Deal with Demakis | Tara Pammi |
| The Ultimate Playboy | Maya Blake |
| Socialite's Gamble | Michelle Conder |
| Her Hottest Summer Yet | Ally Blake |
| Who's Afraid of the Big Bad Boss? | Nina Harrington |
| If Only... | Tanya Wright |
| Only the Brave Try Ballet | Stefanie London |
| Her Irresistible Protector | Michelle Douglas |
| The Maverick Millionaire | Alison Roberts |
| The Return of the Rebel | Jennifer Faye |
| The Tycoon and the Wedding Planner | Kandy Shepherd |
| The Accidental Daddy | Meredith Webber |
| Pregnant with the Soldier's Son | Amy Ruttan |

## MEDICAL

| | |
|---|---|
| 200 Harley Street: The Shameless Maverick | Louisa George |
| 200 Harley Street: The Tortured Hero | Amy Andrews |
| A Home for the Hot-Shot Doc | Dianne Drake |
| A Doctor's Confession | Dianne Drake |

0614GEN STD HB

*Mills & Boon® Large Print*

*July 2014*

# ROMANCE

| | |
|---|---|
| **A Prize Beyond Jewels** | Carole Mortimer |
| **A Queen for the Taking?** | Kate Hewitt |
| **Pretender to the Throne** | Maisey Yates |
| **An Exception to His Rule** | Lindsay Armstrong |
| **The Sheikh's Last Seduction** | Jennie Lucas |
| **Enthralled by Moretti** | Cathy Williams |
| **The Woman Sent to Tame Him** | Victoria Parker |
| **The Plus-One Agreement** | Charlotte Phillips |
| **Awakened By His Touch** | Nikki Logan |
| **Road Trip with the Eligible Bachelor** | Michelle Douglas |
| **Safe in the Tycoon's Arms** | Jennifer Faye |

# HISTORICAL

| | |
|---|---|
| **The Fall of a Saint** | Christine Merrill |
| **At the Highwayman's Pleasure** | Sarah Mallory |
| **Mishap Marriage** | Helen Dickson |
| **Secrets at Court** | Blythe Gifford |
| **The Rebel Captain's Royalist Bride** | Anne Herries |

# MEDICAL

| | |
|---|---|
| **Her Hard to Resist Husband** | Tina Beckett |
| **The Rebel Doc Who Stole Her Heart** | Susan Carlisle |
| **From Duty to Daddy** | Sue MacKay |
| **Changed by His Son's Smile** | Robin Gianna |
| **Mr Right All Along** | Jennifer Taylor |
| **Her Miracle Twins** | Margaret Barker |

# *Mills & Boon® Hardback*
## *August 2014*

# ROMANCE

| | |
|---|---|
| **Zarif's Convenient Queen** | Lynne Graham |
| **Uncovering Her Nine Month Secret** | Jennie Lucas |
| **His Forbidden Diamond** | Susan Stephens |
| **Undone by the Sultan's Touch** | Caitlin Crews |
| **The Argentinian's Demand** | Cathy Williams |
| **Taming the Notorious Sicilian** | Michelle Smart |
| **The Ultimate Seduction** | Dani Collins |
| **Billionaire's Secret** | Chantelle Shaw |
| **The Heat of the Night** | Amy Andrews |
| **The Morning After the Night Before** | Nikki Logan |
| **Here Comes the Bridesmaid** | Avril Tremayne |
| **How to Bag a Billionaire** | Nina Milne |
| **The Rebel and the Heiress** | Michelle Douglas |
| **Not Just a Convenient Marriage** | Lucy Gordon |
| **A Groom Worth Waiting For** | Sophie Pembroke |
| **Crown Prince, Pregnant Bride** | Kate Hardy |
| **Daring to Date Her Boss** | Joanna Neil |
| **A Doctor to Heal Her Heart** | Annie Claydon |

# MEDICAL

| | |
|---|---|
| **Tempted by Her Boss** | Scarlet Wilson |
| **His Girl From Nowhere** | Tina Beckett |
| **Falling For Dr Dimitriou** | Anne Fraser |
| **Return of Dr Irresistible** | Amalie Berlin |

# Mills & Boon® Large Print
## August 2014

# ROMANCE

| | |
|---|---|
| A D'Angelo Like No Other | Carole Mortimer |
| Seduced by the Sultan | Sharon Kendrick |
| When Christakos Meets His Match | Abby Green |
| The Purest of Diamonds? | Susan Stephens |
| Secrets of a Bollywood Marriage | Susanna Carr |
| What the Greek's Money Can't Buy | Maya Blake |
| The Last Prince of Dahaar | Tara Pammi |
| The Secret Ingredient | Nina Harrington |
| Stolen Kiss From a Prince | Teresa Carpenter |
| Behind the Film Star's Smile | Kate Hardy |
| The Return of Mrs Jones | Jessica Gilmore |

# HISTORICAL

| | |
|---|---|
| Unlacing Lady Thea | Louise Allen |
| The Wedding Ring Quest | Carla Kelly |
| London's Most Wanted Rake | Bronwyn Scott |
| Scandal at Greystone Manor | Mary Nichols |
| Rescued from Ruin | Georgie Lee |

# MEDICAL

| | |
|---|---|
| Tempted by Dr Morales | Carol Marinelli |
| The Accidental Romeo | Carol Marinelli |
| The Honourable Army Doc | Emily Forbes |
| A Doctor to Remember | Joanna Neil |
| Melting the Ice Queen's Heart | Amy Ruttan |
| Resisting Her Ex's Touch | Amber McKenzie |

Discover more romance at

# www.millsandboon.co.uk

- ❤ WIN great prizes in our exclusive competitions
- ❤ BUY new titles before they hit the shops
- ❤ BROWSE new books and REVIEW your favourites
- ❤ SAVE on new books with the Mills & Boon® Bookclub™
- ❤ DISCOVER new authors

PLUS, to chat about your favourite reads, get the latest news and find special offers:

- 🟦 Find us on facebook.com/millsandboon
- 🐦 Follow us on twitter.com/millsandboonuk
- ❤ Sign up to our newsletter at millsandboon.co.uk